Abe backed away from the ledge and started up the last fifteen feet to the second overhang. Slowly he inched his way up the gray, cracked granite wall, cautiously groping for fingerholds and toeholds to pull himself up. A moment later Abe was dragging himself onto the overhang. For a minute he sat on the edge, catching his breath and studying the narrow pond below. "It looks a lot higher from up here," he said, pushing himself to his feet. He touched the wall of rock behind him to steady himself.

"You're not chicken, are you?" Travis challenged.

Abe wet his lips. "You sure you don't hit the bottom?"

I shook my head. "It's plenty deep. But you've got to land just right."

All eyes were on Abe. He stood up there for a long time, contemplating the plunge . . .

GHOSTS IN THE BAKER MINE

GHOSTS IN THE BAKER MINE

ALMA J. YATES

Published by
Deseret Book Company
Salt Lake City, Utah

Library of Congress Cataloging-in-Publication Data

Yates, Alma J.
Ghosts in the Baker mine / Alma J. Yates.
p. cm.
Summary: Eleven-year-old Jared's attempt to defend his new friend Abraham from the bullies in his small Mormon town leads to a dangerous incident in an abandoned, supposedly haunted gold mine.
ISBN 0-87579-581-1
[1. Bullies—Fiction. 2. Gold mines and mining—Fiction. 3. Friendship—Fiction. 4. Mormons—Fiction.] I. Title.
PZ7.Y2125Gh 1992
[Fic]—dc20 91-45230
CIP
AC

Printed in the United States of America

10 9 8 7 6 5 4 3 2 1

To Brent R., who had
far more courage than any
of the rest of us.

Chapter 1

Jared," my sister Megan gasped, "Mom says it's time to quit." She had run all four blocks from home to the ball diamond on the southwest corner of the school grounds at Baker Elementary, so her cheeks were red and sweaty. Wearing her faded denim jeans with patched knees, she stopped a few feet from first base, panting, with her hands on her hips and her face screwed up into its meanest glare. I tried to ignore her, but that was hard to do with Megan.

"Jared," she persisted, interrupting the whole game as though none of the other sixth graders were even around.

"Meg," I hissed, scowling in her direction, "not now."

"Mom sent me," she went on, pressing her lips together and trying her best to sprout dimples in her soft, chubby cheeks.

"How's a guy going to play with her running her mouth?" Chris Winder grumbled from the pitcher's mound, his concentration shattered. "Tell her to beat it home."

Megan folded her arms and stubbornly held her ground. I knew right then that she was going to stick with me like some bothersome burr, no matter what anybody said.

I usually didn't mind Megan hanging around. If a guy's got to have a sister—and I have three—he ought to have at least one like Megan. Even for a sister she was cute with her long brown hair that Mom tied in two thick ponytails so that it wouldn't fly all over when she was playing ball, climbing trees, or wrestling with me. She had the biggest, brightest eyes that you could fit into a face and a short, stubby nose, one that she could fit a hundred wrinkles on when she scrunched it up, cocked her head to one side, and asked her dumbest questions.

"Jared Slocombe, I'm not leaving till you come," she warned, bossing like a grown-up instead of the seven-year-old sister she was. "I told Mom I'd get you home," she added, stomping her foot.

"We're ahead," I hissed. "I can't stop now."

Megan's mouth dropped open, and her hands fell to her sides. "You're beating Travis Williams?" Suddenly a huge grin exploded across her face. "Come on, Winder, don't just stand there. Burn that ball across the plate!"

"Slocombe, tell your sister to shut her mouth," Travis Williams growled a dozen feet from the right of home plate. "She's messing up the game, and she's sure getting on my nerves."

Megan frowned in Travis's direction and shouted, "Come on, Jared, you can do it."

Baseball was a big thing in Baker's Bend. It had been for as long as I could remember. I guess in a small town like Baker's Bend there wasn't much else a guy could do. We didn't go to school for math and English and all that other stuff. We just tolerated our studies so that we could race for the ball diamond during recess, lunch hour, and after school.

Travis Williams was the one who was really serious about baseball, talking all the time about making it in the major leagues when he was older. He was the only guy in Baker's Bend who had his own pair of real baseball cleats, and his ball glove cost more than my bike. Of course, his dad owned the biggest ranch in the county and could afford things like that. And he wanted Travis to play in the majors too. That's why he had kept Travis out of school a year so that he would be the oldest kid in the class instead of the youngest. Being the oldest, Travis figured when we played ball he could be the boss of everybody at Baker Elementary. Besides, it was his two bats and ball that we usually used.

"Come on, Winder," I shouted nervously from first base as Chris got ready to throw the next pitch. Chris licked his lips and adjusted his ragged baseball cap over his blond hair. Swallowing once, he glanced over at me. His clear blue eyes were full of worry. I nodded and rasped, "Just one more and he's out. You can do it."

For months I had wanted to beat Travis's team. He figured he was unbeatable. Of course, he made sure he always ended up with Wesley Payton, Skip Manning, and Trevor Malone—the school hotshots, and all bullies besides. Travis didn't care who else ended up on his team as long as he had those three. And I wouldn't have wanted any of the four, even if it had meant winning. The other guys who played with Travis liked to win, but I don't think they cared all that much for Travis as a person.

Before Wesley moved to town two years earlier, Travis had only tried to be the boss when we played ball, but when Wesley arrived, the two of them started hanging around together and playing the bullies all the time. Since they were the biggest and the strongest guys in our grade, they usually managed to get their way. Skip and Trevor joined up with them to form a gang of four.

Most of the guys on my team were the less talented sixth graders, guys that didn't like Travis any more than I did, but they were quiet about it because they were afraid of Travis and Wesley too.

At the beginning of the school year, our team had spent most of our time in the field, chasing Wesley's and Travis's homers, but by spring we were losing by only one or two runs.

Today we had struggled through the first innings, but we never fell behind more than a run or two. Then I hit a homer and knocked two guys in, and we went up by one.

"Don't you strike out, Malone," Travis growled at Trevor.

"Yeah, Malone," Wesley Payton joined in. "We're not losing to these wimps."

Chris Winder suddenly threw the ball. It raced across home plate. Trevor swung. And missed!

All of us in the field let out a holler and threw our gloves into the air.

"Don't dance too soon," Travis growled out at us. "That's only our second out. Wesley's batting now."

Wesley Payton strutted to the plate with a huge grin wrapped around his freckled face. He was the biggest kid in sixth grade and even claimed he had to use his dad's razor once a week. He dusted his hands in the dirt, rubbed them together, and then wiped them on his pants. If anyone could knock the ball all the way to the back steps of the school building behind us, it was Wesley.

"Hey, Payton can't bat now," Chris protested from the pitcher's mound. "It's Skip's turn to bat."

"Skip hurt his leg," Travis laughed. "Didn't you, Skip?"

Skip Manning, a wiry kid with red hair and a big mouth that rarely stopped moving, grinned and nodded his head as he moaned and faked a limp along the sidelines.

"Somebody's got to bat for poor Skip," Travis shrugged.

"It doesn't have to be Wesley," Chris challenged. "You're cheating."

Travis took several steps onto the diamond toward Chris. "Who you calling a cheater?" he demanded.

Chris gulped and glanced in my direction. Travis turned his gaze on me. "You got something to say about that, Slocombe?" he grumbled.

I stared at the ground, anger and frustration rumbling inside me. I looked up once, really quick. All eyes were on me, as though I was the one who had to make this decision. I had felt those staring eyes before, always haunting me, asking me to stand up to Travis. But I couldn't do that. Twice Travis had proved that to me.

"They can't cheat like that, Jared?" Meg spoke up.

"If someone's hurt on my team," Travis asked, "who decides who plays for him, Slocombe?"

I stared at him. "The captain," I answered bitterly.

"I'm the captain," Travis shrugged.

"Skip ain't hurt," I muttered.

Travis laughed. “Sure he is. Just look how he’s limping.”

I looked at Travis. His thick blond hair was pushed up under his new Chicago Cubs baseball cap and his clear blue eyes taunted me. He was handsome. Even guys like me who didn’t like him had to admit that. All the girls seemed to like him, even though he was stuck on himself.

“Let him bat,” I mumbled, smashing a clenched fist into my worn baseball glove.

“He can’t do that, Jared,” Megan protested.

I tried to ignore her, but Megan wasn’t exactly the kind of sister a guy could ignore.

“He’s cheating, Jared. He always cheats.”

“Look, Slocombe,” Travis bristled, “I’m going to chase that sassy little sister of yours all the way to—”

“She can cheer,” I cut him off. “If Payton can bat, Meg can cheer.”

Chris threw the first pitch. Wesley swung and missed. All of us in the field cheered. Wesley reached down and picked up another handful of dirt and let it sift through his fingers. “I won’t miss again,” he muttered. He let the next two pitches go. On the fourth pitch he made a vicious cut at the ball and caught a tiny piece of it. The ball popped up and fell twenty feet behind his team.

“Come on, Chris,” I coaxed, feeling the excitement rising again. “You can do it. Just one more.”

I glanced quickly about the field. Everyone on my team was tense and leaning forward, eyes riveted on Wesley. The red brick, two-story school building was behind us, deserted at four-thirty in the afternoon. There were no spectators to witness our victory, except Meg and Abraham O'Hara, the new kid, who sat on the back steps of the school and silently watched, as he did every afternoon.

"You better not strike out, Payton," Travis threatened.

Wesley gripped his bat. "I'm not going to strike out," he muttered.

Chris wound up for the next pitch. I caught my breath. Chris threw. Wesley swung, putting all his weight into it. The ball was a little outside, but Payton got a good piece of it. There was a loud crack, and the ball fired over my head back toward the school. I stepped to first base to see if the ball would drop in bounds. The ball made it almost to the back steps of the school, but when it landed, it was just a hair outside the invisible out-of-bounds line.

"Foul ball!" I called out excitedly, whipping around and grinning.

"Foul ball nothing," Travis contradicted. "It landed right on the line! Run, Payton, run."

"It's a foul," I protested as Payton ran past me.

"It landed in and bounced out," Travis insisted. "Run, Payton."

"Jared said it was out," Chris called out.

"Slocombe's cross-eyed," Travis came back.

I watched Wesley Payton stroll across home plate, tying the score. I looked back over my shoulder where the ball lay just a few feet from the back steps of the school.

Abraham O'Hara pushed himself up from the steps, walked over to the ball, picked it up, and started toward us. He was the only sixth grader in the whole school who didn't play ball with us, but ever since he'd showed up in Baker's Bend three weeks earlier, he had sat on the back steps of the school and watched every one of our games.

"I got something to say," Abraham spoke up timidly as he approached the infield. All of us stared at him curiously. He was a skinny kid with long sandy brown hair hanging down into his narrow face and growing over his protruding ears. He had a long nose, a pointed chin, and dark suspicious eyes framed by a pair of wire-rimmed glasses that were constantly sliding down his nose and that he was always pushing back with his middle finger.

The first day he'd showed up in Baker's Bend, Mrs. Friedman, the only Jewish lady in town, brought him to class. He had crept into the room with his eyes as big as saucers and his hands stuffed deep in his patched, baggy pants. Wearing an oversized, faded flannel shirt and a ragged canvas Boy Scout belt cinched tightly around his thin waist, he didn't say anything to anybody as he timidly made his way to the desk across the aisle from me.

During morning recess that first day, I discovered him in the restroom crying—about what I never knew. He cried once in class in the afternoon, and all the students snickered and shook their heads, wondering about this weird new kid. No one could remember a sixth grader actually crying in class, especially not one of the guys. Then Abraham found one of Mr. Preston's books, *Amazing Scientific Discoveries*. He buried his face in it and was lost in his own world the rest of the day. Everybody started calling him Professor because of the way he wore his glasses and because he was always reading. Not storybooks, either. He read encyclopedias, science books, history books—boring books like that.

"I saw where it landed," Abraham said, looking back toward the school. "There's a clump of dandelions back there."

"There's dandelions all over this field," Travis grumbled. "Throw us the ball, Professor."

"It was close to the line, no question about that, but it was a foul ball."

Travis laughed. "Professor, you're as cross-eyed as Slocombe. You don't even know what we're playing, let alone whether the ball was foul or fair. Toss us the ball, and go finish reading the dictionary."

"He at least saw where it landed," I protested. "He was the closest one to the ball."

"*I* know where it landed."

"Jared," Megan burst out, "he's a big fat cheater."

"Slocombe, I'm warning you about her mouth," Travis called out, his face turning red and his eyes narrowing.

"Nobody tells me what to do with my mouth," Megan came back, stomping her foot. "Especially not cheaters like you."

"Slocombe!"

"Cheater, cheater, cheater!" Megan taunted.

Travis moved toward Megan. I jumped between them, dropping my mitt. "You going to start beating up little girls now?" I asked.

"Tell her to keep her mouth shut, or I'll start on her big brother."

"I don't tell her anything. She can say what she wants."

Travis walked toward me until his face was inches from mine. Suddenly his hands shot out and hit me full in the chest, taking me completely off guard. I stumbled backward, bumping into Meg and losing my balance. Staggering, I dropped to one knee and then scrambled to my feet again. Travis charged me, giving me a hard shove before I could steady myself. I tripped over my heels and fell on my back. Travis stood over me and pointed down at me. "Don't push your luck,

Slocombe, or I'm going to do more than knock you down." He looked around him. "It was a fair ball. The score's tied."

I stared at Travis. Slowly I pushed myself to my feet, picked up my mitt and muttered, "I've got chores to do."

"You're not going to finish the game?" Travis called to me.

"It's a tie. I've got to get going."

Everyone started leaving. Chris Winder walked over to me. "You okay, Jared?" he asked.

I nodded, brushing at my pants. "One of these days he's going to push me too far."

Chris nodded, but I knew he didn't believe me. I didn't believe myself. I'd fought Travis twice in my life and both times he had beaten me badly. The last time, six months ago, he had left me with a split lip, a bloody nose, and a swollen eye. That fight was over a baseball game too. When she found out, Mom had threatened to drive over and confront Mrs. Williams, but I talked her out of it. I figured if a sixth grader couldn't handle his own fights without dragging his mom into it, he was better off dead.

"We almost had them today," Chris grinned, changing the subject. "We never tied them before."

"We beat them today," I snapped. "One of these days we're going to beat Travis and he's going to stay beat."

"Hey, do you want to go swimming up the canyon Saturday?" Chris asked, grinning. "I'll bet it's warm enough now, even up Baker Canyon."

"I'll have to get my chores done first."

"We'll wait for you up at the pond."

Chapter 2

"You shouldn't let Travis cheat," Megan accused fiercely, tagging along and carrying my glove as we both headed across the grass toward the school while everyone else started for home.

I stopped and Megan, who was right on my heels, bumped into me. "Meg, go home. I've still got to do my janitor work with Mr. Barnes." Every afternoon I earned a couple dollars from Clyde Barnes, the school custodian, helping him clean classrooms and carry out trash.

Megan's eyes narrowed. "Mom's not going to like it that you ran off and played baseball without helping Mr. Barnes first."

I shrugged and started for the school, heaving a sigh and looking about me. Baker's Bend was a pretty place with its huge sycamore trees lining both sides of the streets, stretching their branches across the pavement and making green, leafy tunnels. There weren't any sidewalks in town, just dirt and gravel paths between people's yards and the street. Along the main road through town were two gas stations, the post office, Mack's Grocery and Hardware Store, and Bill Thompson's barber shop that doubled as his insurance office. Everything else in town was just houses, yards, and gardens, except the school on the south and the church with its tall white steeple on the north.

Baker's Bend had about everything I could want, though – good climbing trees, lots of grass and shade, a decent ball park at the school, and Mack's market, where I could load up on soda pop and ice cream sandwiches if I had a little extra money jingling in my pocket. And then there were the mountains east of town, towering tall, rough and rugged and covered with sagebrush, cedars, pines, and maple trees.

Nearly all of the nine hundred people living in Baker's Bend either owned farms west and north of town or worked in the huge moulding mill outside of Fairview, thirteen miles away, which to me was the big city with its twelve thousand people.

"It was a foul ball. No question about it," Abraham O'Hara spoke unexpectedly as I started up the back steps. I looked up, startled from my silent musing. Abraham sat on the top step with his books next to him. He shrugged. "Like I said, it landed just left of that patch of dandelions," he explained, pointing.

"It doesn't make any difference now," I mumbled.

Megan stood at the bottom of the steps with her nose all wrinkled and her head cocked to one side.

"Who's he?" she asked, pointing at Abraham and coming up the steps to stand next to me.

Without answering, I pulled open the heavy wooden back door and walked into Baker Elementary. Staring down the hall with its thickly varnished hardwood floors and high ceilings, I spotted Mr. Barnes's cleaning cart just outside Mrs. Wheatley's third-grade class. I hesitated a moment and then went to a door on my right and pulled it open. A darkened flight of stairs stretched below me. Flipping a light switch, I started down.

"You going to box?" Megan shouted after me. "Mom's going to be plenty mad, Jared Slocombe, when she finds out that you've just been playing ball and boxing when you should have been—"

I ignored her and clomped down the creaky wooden stairs into the musty depths of the Baker School basement, making my way past the boxes, the old desks and chairs, the wooden crates, and the worn-out typewriters and outdated office machines that were all stored down there. I didn't stop until I reached the very back corner of the basement and the old coal bin with black coal stains still scratched into its cement walls.

I pulled open the coal bin door and flipped on the switch just inside. A dim yellow light brightened up the dark interior.

"Wait, Jared," Megan whined behind me. "Don't walk so fast."

A burlap sack stuffed with rags hung from the coal bin ceiling. Mr. Barnes had helped me hang it there months ago, the day I'd found the two pairs of leather boxing gloves inside a dusty cardboard box on top of the abandoned coal furnace. Now those two pairs of scarred gloves lay in the corner of the coal bin. I pulled on a pair and began lashing out at the burlap bag, jabbing and punching and slugging, imagining that the bag was Travis, until sweat broke out on my forehead and trickled down the sides of my face.

"Maybe you ought to forget about baseball," Megan commented behind me. "Maybe you ought to become a boxer. They make millions of dollars just to beat somebody up. I wish you'd beat Travis up. Boxers even get money when somebody beats them up. You'd be a mean boxer, Jared. Nobody could beat you. Nobody. And even if they could, you'd still make loads of money just to let them knock you around a while."

"So this is where you went," a voice exclaimed.

Surprised, I whipped around. Abraham stood in the door. I swallowed and wiped my forehead with the back of my glove.

"What you doing?" he asked.

"Practicing."

"He's going to be a professional boxer," Megan announced. "And he's going to be real rich."

"You're lucky that's just a bag," Abraham commented, grinning, "or you'd get your teeth jarred loose."

I glared at him. "What would you know about it?" I grumbled, slamming my fist into the burlap bag.

I had thought Abraham strange the very first day Mr. Preston led him to the desk across the aisle from me. He lived with Reuben and Ruth Friedman, who were about the only people in Baker's Bend who weren't Mormons. They were Jews, and plenty strange too, living all alone in their two-story brick house just down the street from me. They didn't even celebrate Christmas and Easter, and that was enough to convince me that they were weird.

"I was going to box once," Abraham remarked.

"You?" I asked doubtfully. He nodded. "So now you're an expert because once you thought you might box?"

"I had a brother who was a Golden Gloves champion."

I wasn't sure what a Golden Gloves champion was, but I wasn't going to let Abraham know that.

"He showed me a few things. I used to go to the gym where he worked out. I didn't ever miss any of his fights. He had thirty-three knock-outs."

I turned and started on the bag again.

"You need to lead more with your left. Then when something opens up, you go in with the right. Your left should be your battering ram. Your right is your bone crusher. But you've got to hold your left up more to guard your face and hold your elbows in to guard your body. And keep moving. Dance around. Don't let anybody draw a bead on you. And watch out for–"

"Hey, Professor, I know what I'm doing."

Abraham stopped in midsentence, his mouth open. He stared at me and then shrugged. "I just thought you might want some pointers," he said, subdued.

I returned to the burlap bag.

"Does everybody let Travis Williams boss them around?" Abraham asked unexpectedly.

I stopped punching and turned back to Abraham, my arms drooping at my sides.

"Jared doesn't let anybody boss *him* around," Megan spoke up. "He could've busted Travis's nose, but Mom doesn't like him fighting. He'd get a whipping when he got home if he beat up on Travis. That's why he didn't fight out there."

Abraham looked at Megan and smiled. Shaking his head, he remarked, "You could have won today if you hadn't backed down. The ball game, I mean."

"Who cares about baseball?" I muttered.

"Do you figure you could beat Travis? In a fight?"

"It's not something I think a lot about," I lied, turning back to the burlap bag.

"Jared could beat anybody in Baker's Bend," Megan defended me.

"I figure that he'd be a tough one to handle, but if a guy knew what he was doing—"

"Do you always push your nose into everybody's business?" I cut him short, feeling my face burn with anger and embarrassment.

Abraham pulled off his glasses and began polishing them with his shirt tail.

"You figure you could beat Travis?" Abraham asked. "With those?" he added, nodding toward my gloves.

"I could beat you."

He laughed, shaking his head. "I doubt it. Not from what I've seen."

I stomped over to the corner, snatched up the other pair of gloves and tossed them to Abraham. "Put them on, tough guy. Let's see how good *you* are."

He smiled and examined the gloves. "These are old ones, aren't they?"

"They'll do."

"I haven't seen gloves like these for a long time. The ones we used in the gym in Philadelphia were new. They were the kind the pros use."

"Just put them on. Let's see if you can use your fists as good as you can use your mouth."

"I don't fight." He shrugged, tossing the gloves

back to me. "I made a promise," he added. "I told my mom I wouldn't fight."

"You'd just be giving me a few pointers. Since you're so good," I added, angry.

He thought a moment and then nodded. "All right. I'll try not to hurt you."

"Don't try too hard," I muttered.

He handed his glasses to Megan, pulled the gloves on, and faced me. I had never wanted to punch anybody as much as I wanted to punch Abraham O'Hara right then. I knew that beating a guy like Abraham was nothing to brag about, but I'd do it down in the basement where no one would see, and I could at least shut up his face.

With my fists up I crossed the coal bin, charging toward him. He grinned and slipped away from me, dancing lightly on his toes and moving in a circle just beyond my reach. He kept his fists in front of him, jabbing at me every two or three seconds, but he was always too far away to do anything but thump harmlessly on my gloves.

"Stand still!" I ordered. "We're boxing, not playing tag."

He grinned and shook his head. "A good boxer always keeps on the move. Then when something opens up—Pow! He goes for it."

Angry, I charged him, letting my guard down. I threw a wild punch, and suddenly my whole head exploded into a flash of yellow lights. Abraham had caught me with a right hook on the bridge of my nose. My eyes began to water, and my knees wobbled.

"You didn't expect that one, did you?" Abraham laughed. "You let your guard down."

I shook my head, clamped my jaw tight, and moved in, cautious and more determined than ever. I forced him to a corner and then closed in before he could slip away. This time I didn't let my guard down. Abraham saw the trap. His eyes widened and he darted for my left, but I closed in on him, throwing an angry right punch that caught him on the side of the face and sent him crashing into the cement wall. I threw another punch that caught him full in the face, snapping his head back.

Staggering and finally dropping to his knees, he stripped off his gloves and held the back of his head. A slow trickle of blood came from his nose.

My anger drained from me when I saw his bloody nose. "You okay?" I asked, suddenly worried that I might have hurt him.

"I knew I shouldn't have fought," he moaned. "I promised." His face was pale and his oversized Adam's apple bobbed in his throat as he swallowed and tried to catch his breath.

"You okay?" I ventured guiltily. "I didn't mean to hurt you," I lied. "I mean, I didn't think I'd bloody your nose and bang your head into the wall. You going to be okay?"

Slowly he tried to push himself up and then sank back to the floor with a groan.

"He's littler than you, Jared," Megan spoke up accusingly. She crept over and knelt beside Abraham, putting her small hand on his shoulder.

Abraham touched his nose with the tip of his finger. Continuing to moan softly, he bent over with one hand on the back of his head and the other holding his nose. He started to stand again.

"Maybe you shouldn't get up yet. I wasn't meaning to hit you so hard." Leaning over him and seeing how skinny he was, I felt guilty. "You talked like you knew what you were doing, though."

"I *know* what I'm supposed to do," he whined. "I just don't do it sometimes." I could tell he was disgusted with himself.

"I've got work to do upstairs," I muttered, throwing my gloves into the corner.

A few minutes later I was in Mr. Preston's room wiping down the blackboard, angry with myself for beating up on a guy like Abraham O'Hara. I wished that Megan hadn't been there to see it. I could tell that my fighting had upset her because she hadn't bragged on me like she usually did; instead, she had stayed behind in the coal bin to help Abraham.

"Do you need some help, Jared?" Abraham called

unexpectedly from the door, the dried traces of blood still on his lip and smeared across his cheek. Megan stood behind him.

I faced him. "Why'd you make me believe that you knew something about boxing?"

He wet his lips and got a pinched, uneasy look on his face. "I know a lot about boxing. My brother Isaac taught me."

"He was the Golden Gloves champion?"

He nodded. "He said I had potential. He claimed I had the stuff to be a better boxer than he was." He shook his head. "But I don't want to be a boxer." He was quiet a moment. "I could be a trainer, though. I get nervous when I'm the one doing the boxing. But I can tell someone else what to do."

"You ought to go and wash your face. It looks like the bleeding's stopped."

Abraham went across the hall to the restroom, and I returned to my cleaning. A few minutes later, without my even asking him, Abraham returned and started hauling trash, wiping blackboards, and pushing a broom. I didn't really want him hanging around and helping, but I felt sorry for him after I'd beaten up on him like I had, so I let him help me.

Chapter 3

The sun was dropping rapidly, sending long shadows everywhere, when Abraham and I finally left the school with Megan tagging behind.

"I've never been in a place like Baker's Bend," Abraham commented as we ambled across the school's lawn and started up Miner Street toward my place four blocks away. "Philly has over a million people. How did Baker's Bend ever start clear out here?"

I shrugged. "The Mormons settled it a hundred years ago and named it Calls Fort. All they were looking for was a place to farm. The town was never much until old Horace Baker and his brother Jake started their gold mine. Then new people moved in and changed the name to Baker's Bend."

"Baker's Bend was a mining town?"

"Long before I was ever around."

"I used to live in a mining town," Abraham commented. "I didn't always live in Philly. It was a coal mine, though." He shrugged. "Where's Jake and Horace's mine?"

I pointed to the mountain. "Almost to the top. Actually there are a half dozen or more of them."

"Nobody's supposed to go in those mines," Megan spoke up. "They're haunted. Packed full of ghosts and things."

Abraham looked down at Megan and laughed. "Mines don't have ghosts."

Megan looked up at him like he'd sprouted a second head. "The Baker Mine does," she insisted.

"You figure there are ghosts up there?" he asked, turning to me and ignoring Megan.

I swallowed hard. I didn't know anybody in Baker's Bend that wasn't spooked some by the mines. Even the old people. I had been up there with some of the guys in town, mainly on dares. Mom and Dad had threatened to lock me in my room for a week if I prowled around the mines, but I had gone a few times anyway without their knowing it. I had walked past the leaning "Keep Out" signs posted in front and even ventured a few feet inside the black hole of the main mine. I had peered down the dark, dank passage and shouted and laughed to hear the dull, dead echo. But my laugh had always made the hair curl on the back of my neck and made my stomach flip-flop inside me.

"Have you ever been to the back of the mine?" I had asked Dad one day while we were working in the yard.

Without smiling he had looked at me and said

quietly, "I wouldn't want to go to the back of the mine."

"Wouldn't you like to know what it's like?"

"It's a dangerous place, Jared. Don't go up there."

"Do you figure it's haunted?"

"In its own way."

I turned to Abraham. "I just know what different people—"

"Those mines are packed clear full of ghosts and dead men's bones," Megan interrupted. "Sometimes at night while I'm lying in bed, I can hear the ghosts howling and screaming clear down here. And I have the window closed too."

"Megan, you're talking crazy," I growled.

"Well, I can," she came back fiercely.

Abraham laughed. "I don't believe in ghosts."

I kicked at a rock and sent it bouncing and rolling down the street in front of us. "I don't know what's up there. Not for sure. I mean, some people claim there are ghosts in the Baker Mine." I scratched the back of my neck. "There are stories about—"

"There are always stories about abandoned mines. Every abandoned mine is supposed to have its own pack of ghosts. There's nothing to those stories, though." He grinned. "People tell them just to scare little girls."

"I'm not a little girl!" Megan flared. "The Baker Mine caved in and swallowed up a bunch of miners.

They're still buried up there. At least their ghosts are."

"Is that what everybody says?"

I didn't answer right away. I continued walking down Miner Street, shuffling my feet and staring down at the black pavement criss-crossed with tiny cracks. "Travis Williams went in with his uncle Blaine," I announced, looking up. "His uncle is a sergeant in the marines. He's earned medals and everything. He and Travis planned to go to the very back of the mine. Blaine claimed that the mine wasn't haunted, that it was just a hole in the ground. But they didn't make it to the back." I looked over at Abraham as we walked along. Megan reached up and took my hand and huddled closer.

"Travis says they heard noises. He figured it was ghosts screaming. Not even Travis's uncle Blaine wanted to stay in that mine. He said it was like someone was following them in there, just waiting for them to get far enough inside so they couldn't get out again. He had his pistol and a hunting knife, but what good are they against ghosts?"

Abraham smiled and shook his head. "That doesn't prove anything."

"Ernie Dobson—he's a grown man—rode up Baker Canyon. He was planning to go into the mine. He claimed he wasn't afraid. But he said the whole time he was riding up there he thought someone was watching him. He said he could feel their eyes on him. He tied his horse to a tree—tied it real good. He walked into the mine, just a few feet away, and then got spooked. He left the mine on a run and went back to where he'd left his horse. It was gone, the reins cut." I swallowed and took a deep breath. "He went charging down that mountain. He's a good climber, Ernie is. But he fell that day. Broke a leg and both his wrists. And he didn't find his horse. Not for nearly a year. One day while Roger Perkins was climbing in Baker's Canyon he found a pile of horse bones and Ernie's saddle at the foot of a cliff in a mess of tangled bushes."

"What does that prove?"

"There's something up there," I snapped, running out of patience. "People have camped up there in the canyon, and things end up missing when there's nobody around to take them. People hurt themselves when they wouldn't hurt themselves any other place."

"Well," Abraham said, shrugging, "you can believe in ghosts and things if you want. Not me."

"Abraham, what made you come to Baker's Bend?" I asked, changing the subject.

"You can call me Abe. I'd rather you didn't call me Professor, though."

"That 'Professor' slipped out back there at the school. I was mad."

"You mind if I play baseball with you sometime?"

I looked over at him. "Do you know how?"

"Shoot! I played all the time in Philadelphia. They had lots of teams back there. Now *they* know how to play ball."

"Do you play baseball like you box?"

"I *play* baseball."

"You don't just talk about it?"

Abe pushed his glasses up his nose and kept walking. "Boxing makes me nervous. I don't like to get hit."

"Are Reuben and Ruth Friedman friends of yours?" I asked.

"My aunt and uncle."

I stopped, shocked. "Your aunt and uncle? But they're Jews," I burst out.

Abe stopped and looked me over like I'd just popped out of the ground from a seed. "What difference does that make?"

I shrugged, pushing my hands into my pockets.

"Uncle Reuben is my mom's older brother."

"What makes them Jews?" Megan asked, her eyes big with wonder.

Abe glanced at Megan. "They were just born that way."

"You mean you can be born a Jew?"

"How else would you get to be one?"

"Are *you* a Jew?" I asked, my mouth dropping open.

"With a little Gentile thrown in."

"What's *Gentile?*" Megan wondered, scrunching up her nose. "It sounds like some kind of lizard. Is that worse than being a Jew?"

"Jews think so. You're a Gentile."

Megan shook her head. "I'm an American and a Mormon. I ain't no Gentile."

Abe took a deep breath and let it out as a heavy sigh. "You are as far as Jews are concerned."

"Well, I don't have to ask any old Jew what I am."

"So your mom was a Jew?" I asked.

"Until she married my dad. Her family were pretty strict Jews. Her grandfather was a rabbi."

"A what?" Megan spoke up.

"That's like a Jewish priest or minister. When Mom married Dad, her family had a funeral for her."

"Even before she was really dead? Just because she married your dad?"

Abe nodded. "Jews are supposed to marry Jews. When she didn't marry a Jew, her family didn't want anything to do with her. Or Isaac and me."

"So you're a Jew?"

"Half and half. My dad was Irish Catholic."

"Then how did you end up with your mom's brother?"

"Uncle Reuben almost married a Gentile himself. He didn't go to Mom's Jewish funeral."

"So you're a Jew but you became a Catholic?"

Abe shook his head. "I don't know much more about being a Jew than you. And I don't know anything about being a Catholic."

The sun was beginning to set as we came to the last block on Miner Street. I turned left at the corner.

"Why are you turning?" Abe asked me, puzzled. "Don't you live just up past Uncle Reuben's?"

"Sure we do," Megan blurted out, "but there's no way we're going by Loco Leo's place. Not when it's starting to get dark."

"Loco Leo?"

I stared down the street at the old Mansion halfway down the block. Horace Baker had built it. At one time it had been the fanciest place in Baker's Bend. Maybe the fanciest place in the whole county. After the mine folded, a few people lived in it off and on, but no one stayed long. Gradually it was abandoned until Leon Lucero moved in a few years back.

Leon, or Loco Leo as we kids called him, was old and bent over, always sneaking about with a gnarled walking stick or driving around town in his beatup, black pickup truck, collecting junk from everywhere.

I swallowed. I never passed the Mansion alone when shadows were beginning to creep and crawl everywhere. Sometimes a bunch of us would go by and shout things at Loco Leo or throw rocks at his house and run. Sometimes he would shout back. Most of the time he would just stand in his window, glaring after us, casting some mysterious spell with his stony stare.

"I usually take the long way and cut through the block," I explained. I started down the street, and Abe followed.

"You scared of Leo?" Abe asked matter-of-factly.

"Well, who isn't?" Megan burst out. "He's crazy. And he spent about fifty years in prison."

"How do you know?" Abe demanded.

"He just did," I answered, stopping and facing Abe. "He used to beat his wife and his four daughters. They left him and went someplace in the northern part of the state, but he went after them. I'm not sure what he did when he found them, but they sent him to prison for it. When he got out, he never could find his family. He was crazy mean after that, always drinking and fighting. Dad said Leo's spent more time in jail than any man in the whole country.

"One night in Fairview he was drunk and got in a fight with some ranch hand. He tore the whole place up. Before it was over, he had killed the guy. Hit him in the head with a chair. The next morning, when he was sober again, he claimed he couldn't even remember doing it. That's how crazy he was. But they sent him to prison anyway. He was there for ten years or so."

"Are those just stories too, like the ghosts in the mine?"

"I remember when he moved back to Baker's Bend. He was fresh out of prison. I was five or six then." I glanced back at the Mansion and licked my lips. "One night I woke up. It was late. Police lights were flashing in front of the Mansion, and I could hear shouting and screaming. I thought there had been an accident or something. I sneaked out of bed and headed that way. I'd never seen an accident and figured it would be pretty exciting." I shook my head.

"After, I wished I had stayed in bed. I couldn't sleep the rest of the night. Or a lot of nights after that. There were three patrol cars there, two from Fairview. The officers were dragging Loco Leo out of the Mansion. He was kicking and screaming that they weren't ever going to take him back to prison. He said they'd have to kill him first. It took five policemen to get him handcuffed and locked in the back of the police car. Then he kicked the window out. He was a crazy man. I know it for sure. I saw it with my own eyes. That was the third time Loco Leo got sent to prison." I shrugged. "He was only there a year or so that time, though."

"What made Leo come to Baker's Bend in the first place?"

"He grew up here. He's the only guy still around that worked for Horace Baker in the mine. He wasn't much older than me and you when the mines were running, but he helped haul supplies up the mountain on pack mules. He could tell some stories that would make your blood freeze in your veins."

"Yeah," Megan added. "Horace Baker's wife hung herself in the very house where Loco Leo lives right now. He's got to be crazy to live in a place like that."

"Now all he does is snoop around picking up junk," I said.

"Uncle Reuben says a guy can make lots of money collecting scrap iron and such. He's got a friend in Fairview that's a millionaire from collecting the same kind of stuff."

"You mean Jesse the Jew is a friend of your uncle Reuben?"

"Jesse Stein," Abe corrected. "Being a Jew isn't like having a disease or anything."

"Well, Loco Leo isn't a Jew," Megan spoke up. "He's crazy mean. I'll bet you wouldn't dare walk up on his porch some dark night and knock."

"I've been to his place. Once."

"You're a liar," I accused.

Abe shook his head. "Aunt Ruth sent me with an old pick Uncle Reuben had borrowed."

"Did you go inside his house?"

"I went up on his porch."

"Did you see inside?" I asked.

Abe shook his head.

"He's got places in his basement where he can

lock people up and torture them," Megan said. "That's what he did to his wife and daughters. That's why they ran away."

Abe laughed and looked down at the gravel along the side of the road. His long straight hair hung down in his eyes, and he brushed it away with his hand. "I'm not afraid of old men and houses or broken down mines that are supposed to be full of ghosts." Without saying another word, he turned back to Miner Street, leaving Megan and me behind.

"He's weird," Megan commented as we watched him march past the Mansion.

"Let's go home, Megan," I spoke softly. "Mom will be wondering where we are."

Chapter 4

Our yellow frame house with its white window shutters stood at the edge of town and rested quietly beneath two huge willow trees with a small lawn in front. The foot of the mountain with its blue sage and cedar trees was our backyard. The driveway, a long gravel lane branching off the end of Miner Street, was lined with a barbed wire fence, giant poplar trees, and patches of wild, tangled currant bushes.

Our nearest neighbors were the Friedmans, nearly a block away. Being away from everyone gave us the chance to have the makings of a small farm – a garden plot, a couple of corrals for our two cows and mare, a leaning wooden shed that served as a chicken coop, and a gray, weatherworn barn full of hay and straw where we did the milking.

Darkness had closed in when I finally finished milking our two cows and feeding the chickens. I was later than usual as I lugged my bucket brimming with foaming milk from the barn and headed for the back porch to strain the milk before taking it inside.

"Hey, Jared," someone called to me. I stopped and looked around.

"Hello, Uncle Josh," I called back, setting my milk pail down and grinning a greeting. "What brings you over tonight?" Then I saw that Uncle Josh was wearing his dark suit and packing a black binder under his arm. I knew right away that he was doing his bishop work.

Uncle Josh smiled and slapped me on the back. "Heard anything from your dad?"

"Mom got a letter yesterday." I brightened up. "He'll finish his job in Arizona by the end of May. Then he'll be home for good."

"He better be. I know a young man who needs to be ordained a deacon the end of May."

I became serious. "I wish he could come home sooner."

"You like to eat, don't you?"

I nodded.

"By the middle of June, Fairview Moulding Mill will be back in full operation, and your dad can stay home." Uncle Josh put his arm around my shoulders and squeezed. "You've done a good job filling in for him."

I bent over, reached for the milk bucket, and started for the house. "Did you want to see Mom?"

Shaking his head, he answered, "I'm on my way to the church, but I dropped by to see you."

I stopped and turned.

"Bishop's business," he said simply. "There's a new boy in town. Abraham O'Hara."

I stared for a moment, setting the milk bucket down again.

"What do you know about him?" asked Uncle Josh.

"He's different, that's for sure."

"I didn't realize until today that he was even in town. I spoke with his branch president from Pennsylvania on the phone this morning."

I stared at Uncle Josh. "Abe? A Mormon? He can't be."

"I learned quite a bit about that young man. I'm just sorry that it's taken me so long to discover him. He's needed us before now." Uncle Josh rubbed his black binder, thinking deeply. "A few years ago his father was killed. He had an older brother who was stabbed to death in a street fight. His mother died of cancer just before he came out here. Except for his Uncle Reuben, his mother's family won't have anything to do with him. His dad's folks aren't crazy about having Jewish relatives either. He might be turned over to a foster family if Reuben and Ruth decide they can't have him. For a young man who has just turned twelve, he faces some pretty ugly challenges. No one should have to face those alone."

"He didn't say anything about being Mormon."

Uncle Josh shrugged and pushed his hands deep into his pants pockets. "He needs someone, Jared. I feel sorry that he's been here this long and that I haven't even known about him." He paused. "Would you like another friend?"

"I've got plenty of friends."

"It would make a world of difference if Abraham O'Hara had a friend, a good friend."

I fidgeted uneasily. "He's a little weird, Uncle Josh, not like the rest of us. Not that that makes any difference, but–"

"He needs you, Jared. He needs all of us."

I stared at the ground. "I'm not sure what I could do. I mean, I don't think Mom could put him up here, not with Dad gone and all."

"He needs a friend, Jared. A guy can face a lot of challenges in life if he has one good friend to stand by him."

"I don't know of anybody that even likes him. They hassle him some."

"What about you?"

I ducked my head. "I don't bother him much, but I don't have much to do with him, either. I mean, he's got other things to do. He reads his books and stays by himself most of the time." I didn't want to admit right then that I had actually walked home with him today.

"A deacon would look out for someone like Abraham."

"I'm not a deacon."

"You will be by the end of next month."

I shrugged. "Why don't you talk to Travis or Wesley? They're the ones that bug him the most. And they're already deacons. If they backed off, Abraham would be okay."

"Would they be his friends?"

I shook my head. "Probably not. They don't like him."

"Abraham needs you, Jared. A lot of the guys need you."

"Need me? For what?"

"They want somebody to follow, somebody to lean on."

"They've got Travis and Wesley," I mumbled.

Uncle Josh shook his head. "Think about it, Jared. Think about Abraham. And the others."

Uncle Josh ruined my whole night. I didn't want Abe to be a Mormon. I liked him better as just a plain, ordinary, weird Jew, sitting by himself on the back steps of the school with his face buried in a science book, not saying anything and not bothering me. I didn't want Abe to need me. I didn't want anybody to need me. And yet, deep inside I didn't want to be alone.

I fussed over supper and grumbled at Meg for

humming while she ate her peas. After eating, I shut myself in my room so I could study, but I didn't study much. I kept thinking of Abraham O'Hara. I thought of the baseball game and all the eyes staring at me, waiting for me to do something. But what?

Suddenly there was a knock on the door. "Jared," Megan shouted, "can you tuck us in and tell us a story?" Megan turned the knob, pushed open the door, and stood there in her nightgown with her favorite green blanket clutched in her arms.

"I didn't say you could come in," I grumbled.

She grinned, doing her very best to sprout dimples again. "I didn't figure you'd mind. Will you tell us a story?"

"I've got homework, you know."

"I know, but just one story, Jared."

Meg knew I couldn't turn her down. Sometimes I could turn Lauren and Michelle down, but not Meg. That's why she was always the one who came and asked. "One story," I said, trying to sound tough.

Lauren, who was four, and Michelle, who was nine, were already in bed when I went in with Megan. Dad used to be the one to tell the girls their bedtime story, but with him gone Megan had recruited me.

"I can only stay for a little while," I announced.

"Tell us about the Baker Mine," Megan burst out

as she burrowed between her sheets and pulled her green blanket under her chin.

"Mom doesn't like me telling you that story," I muttered as the room became quiet.

"We won't get scared. Promise," Megan whispered. "I didn't get scared when you and that funny boy talked about it today."

I hesitated. "All right, but if you go bawling to Mom—"

I thought a moment. "Well, Horace and Jake Baker found the mine a long time ago. Horace was the brains, the businessman, and he was the one who wanted to be rich, to be the richest man in the world. Jake was the miner, a crazy, ugly, mean old guy with a crooked walking stick and a wolf dog for a pet. He didn't care all that much about the money. He mainly liked the adventure of finding gold. He became the mine foreman and kept to himself most of the time.

"Horace wanted lots of rich things. He built the Mansion and invited all kinds of rich people to Baker's Bend. Some even came from England and France. During the day he took them up the mountain to see his famous gold mines. At night he held big parties and dances in the Mansion so the rich people would pay money to own part of the Baker Mine. Once the governor even came."

"The governor?" Michelle asked. "Were there princes and princesses and people like that?"

"Michelle," I muttered, "This isn't one of those mushy fairy-tale stories. Just listen. There was a lot of gold and a little silver at first and—"

"What about diamonds and rubies?" Megan asked.

"I don't know," I said impatiently. "Maybe they found diamonds and rubies too. Just let me talk. Everybody thought this was going to be the richest mine around. And then one winter the mine caved in, and lots of miners were trapped inside. Horace's own brother Jake was one of them. But Horace didn't care. All he cared about was finding more gold. He didn't even try to dig those miners out. He left them there, hollering and screaming while he went off and dug himself another mine close to the first one. But nothing worked after that because the whole mountain was haunted by those dead miners."

"Was Loco Leo one of them?" Megan asked.

"My friend Connie says Loco Leo is really Jake Baker," Michelle spoke up in a raspy whisper.

"Connie's got bats in her brain," I muttered. "Jake's dead. Now let me finish the way it really happened. I've got homework to do."

I cleared my throat. "Jake's ghost wanders around on the mountain with his half-wolf dog, looking for his brother Horace because he knows Horace left him in the mine to die just so he could keep mining for more gold. And when Jake finds him—"

"But what about Mrs. Baker?" Michelle interrupted. "Wasn't she beautiful and a fancy lady?"

"Do you always have to bring the mush in, Michelle?" I complained. "I don't know anything about her being a lady or beautiful or anything like that. All I know is that she went crazy, climbed up into the top of the Mansion, and hung herself. Grandpa says he remembers when they hauled her out of the Mansion, wrapped in one of her silk sheets."

"And did the governor and the princes and princesses come crying to her funeral and—"

"Oh, brother," I grumbled, starting for the door. "A guy can't even tell a decent ghost story without you trying to turn it into Sleeping Beauty or something else. I've got homework to do."

The next day in school Abe caught me staring across the aisle at him a couple of times, but each time I quickly looked away. As I played ball after school, I kept looking over my shoulder and seeing Abe sitting alone on the back steps. I wished that Uncle Josh hadn't told me anything about Abe. I liked it better when he was just a weird kid that I didn't have to think about.

Travis Williams and his team beat us that afternoon, worse than we had been beaten for weeks. I waited on the ball diamond until the others had left; then I wandered over to the school to put in my hour with Mr. Barnes.

As I started down the hall to the janitor's closet, I heard the back door open and close behind me. "Are you going to box this afternoon?" Abe called after me.

I ignored him.

"I could be your coach."

"I don't need a coach. I can box just fine all by myself."

"You could beat anybody with a good coach."

"A coach like you, I suppose?" I asked, turning to face him.

He grinned. "I figure I'm about the best trainer in all of Baker's Bend."

"When I need a trainer, I'll come looking for you," I mumbled, grabbing a push broom.

Abe shrugged and started working alongside me. "Baker Elementary is a small school, isn't it? That must be the reason they're shutting the place down at the end of the school year. Back in Philly we had more kids in our sixth grade than Baker's got in the whole school."

I glared over at Abe as he wiped down the chalkboard in Mrs. Farley's room. No one in Baker's Bend liked to talk about the closing of Baker Elementary. But it was going to happen. The school board in Fairview was determined. After nearly fifty years, the school was going to close its doors forever.

"It's probably just as well," Abe went on monotonously. "I hear Landon Elementary in Fairview is a bigger and better place."

"Says who?"

Abe glanced about the room and gestured with a sweep of his arm. "Just look at this place. It's a dump. Ready to fall down." He stomped on the floor. "Warped floor boards with two inches of old varnish on them."

"The floors aren't warped."

"In the corner of Mr. Gilbert's room they are."

"That isn't any reason to close the school."

"Old creaky windows and doors," Abe went on. "This place should have been condemned a long time ago."

"I like this school."

"Back in Philly—"

"If Philly was so great," I cut in, suddenly angry, "why did you bother to come out here to Baker's Bend?" I began kicking desks out of the way and pushing my broom along. "Why didn't you stay in Philly where everything was so great?" I looked up. Abe was gone. I kicked at a chair and thought of Uncle Josh.

When I finished my janitor work, I said good-bye to Mr. Barnes and headed out the back door for home. Abe was sitting on the back steps, staring out across the playground. He stood up and started home with me.

"A guy came to see me last night," Abe commented matter-of-factly. "He said he's your uncle."

I nodded. "You didn't say you were a Mormon," I accused.

Abe shook his head. "I was once. I don't think I'm anything now."

"What do you mean?"

"You have to belong someplace to be anything." He shrugged. "I don't know that I belong anyplace."

"You don't want to be a Mormon any more?"

"What good does it do to be a Mormon if no one ever comes for you, if no one's ever there when you need them?"

I didn't answer. I didn't know the answer then. It wouldn't come till later.

Chapter 5

Saturday morning I rushed through my chores so I would have most of the day to myself, but it was almost ten when I finished mucking out the barn. I clomped into the kitchen for a drink.

"Where you off to?" Mom asked as I stood at the sink and gulped my water.

"It's warm out there," I mumbled, wiping my face with the back of my hand. "Good swimming weather." I set my cup down. "Some of the guys are heading up to Baker Canyon."

"To the ponds?" she asked, looking up from the glob of bread dough she was kneading on the kitchen table.

I nodded.

"Jared Slocombe," she warned, shaking a flour-covered finger in my direction, "You be careful. That's where Frank Anderson drowned."

I nodded indifferently. Every time I went to Baker Pond, Mom reminded me of Frank Anderson. Frank had been a year younger than Dad and had drowned when he was fourteen, but the way Mom talked you would have thought it had happened last week.

"Mom, I know how to swim," I reminded her.

"Frank knew how to swim too. But he got to fooling around."

"Frank was trying to shoot the Cave and got stuck. He shouldn't have been dumb enough to shoot the Cave in the first place."

"You just be careful, Jared Slocombe," she cautioned as I went out the front door. "I don't want anyone dragging you out of that pond."

When I left the house, Megan was sitting on the front steps clutching a towel and her swimming suit. "I'm ready, Jared," she announced excitedly.

I stared down at her and shook my head.

"Why not?" she demanded, standing up.

I heaved a sigh. "You can't swim."

"I can wade."

"The place is going to be crawling with guys, Meg. They don't want a girl hanging around."

"What's wrong with a girl hanging around?"

"We've got to get dressed in the bushes and stuff. You just can't have a girl around."

"I won't peek. I'll find another bush."

I shook my head. "And don't follow me up the mountain."

I headed out into the street while Megan stayed behind, pouting on the front porch. I looked back once, and she raised her hand and waved sadly. I felt like a real crumb, but sometimes you just can't take your little sister.

I'd walked only a couple blocks when I heard someone running behind me. I whipped around to scold Meg for following me, but it wasn't Meg.

"Where you headed?" Abe gasped, as he galloped up, brushing the hair from his eyes and squinting into the sun's morning glare.

I held up my old pair of cutoffs and touched the ragged towel I had around my neck. "Swimming," I explained simply.

"Where does a guy swim in Baker's Bend?"

"Up the canyon, in Baker Pond." I nodded toward the mountain.

"Can anybody go?"

I shrugged. "Do you swim?"

Abe grinned and nodded. "I used to swim all the time in Philly. You'd like Philly."

"I kinda like Baker's Bend," I grumbled.

"Hey, if I get something to wear, can I come?"

"You'd have to find the place on your own," I said, not wanting to wait for him and wanting to discourage him from coming along.

"Is there a trail or something?"

"The old mine road is just east of the school. It goes to the mouth of the canyon. There's a trail from there."

Abe thought a moment and then grinned. "I think I can find it. I'll see you up there."

Tall pines, maple trees, and thick brush filled the bottom of Baker Canyon. A few pines and cedars had found cracks and crevices in the craggy canyon walls where they managed to grow. Winding its way along the bottom of the canyon was the old mining trail, which was bordered on the left by Baker Creek and on the right by the steep canyon wall.

A quarter of a mile from the mouth of the canyon was the abandoned ore dump. All that was left from the mining days were a few rotting timbers and rusting scraps of iron, sections of cable and mining track.

The creek splashed and foamed down the rocky canyon bottom and over a ten-foot falls to Baker Pond, which was scrunched between the ore dump and the steep north canyon wall. The pond was fairly narrow, no more than twenty-five feet across at its widest point. A few years after the mines closed, huge slabs of rock and concrete began tumbling into the water, forming a rough bridge and dividing the pond in half.

Even before I reached the pond I could hear the shouts from the others who were at the pond. I broke into a run.

Chris Winder and a half dozen other guys were already there. "It's just right," Chris called out to me as I hurriedly charged into the bushes to change into my cutoffs.

The dark water was icy, and the only way a guy could survive was to jump in all at once and let the piercing cold numb his body senseless. I held my breath, closed my eyes, and made the shocking plunge.

For ten minutes I splashed and swam. Most of our swimming was done in the upper pool, just below the waterfall, where the pool was deep. It was impossible for your eyes to pierce the dark waters from the bank. Even when you jumped from the overhangs along the north wall, you couldn't touch the bottom.

"Who invited the Professor?" I heard someone mutter behind me as I came out of the water, shaking my head, and rubbing my eyes with wet fists. I spotted him dressed in a ragged T-shirt and a shabby pair of Levi's cut off at the knee. Standing on a rock on the south bank, he grinned down at us, looking skinnier and whiter than ever.

"I told him he could come," I answered with a shrug of my shoulders. "What's wrong with that?" I asked, turning to Chris.

Chris stared at him for a moment and then shrugged his shoulders. "Jump in, Professor," he grinned. "If you're not scared."

Abe smiled, pulled his glasses off, set them on a rock, and crept gingerly into the water, hugging himself against the watery chill. Nobody said anything else about Abe being there—until Travis, Wesley, and Trevor showed up half an hour later. Travis didn't pay much attention to who was there until he climbed up the north wall to jump. "Hey," he shouted down. "Where'd the Professor come from?" he snorted. "Did you come up here to read your dictionary or to tell us about baseball?" He laughed.

Abe sat shivering on a rock on the bank. "It was a foul ball the other day," Abe spoke up good-naturedly. "I showed Jared where the ball landed, and sure as anything it was a foul ball." He grinned. "I'll bet they would have beaten you if—"

"Go drown yourself, Professor," Travis snapped. "Nobody needs you telling us how to play ball." I could tell Travis was angry because Abe had brought up the disputed call. "And who said you could come up around here any way?"

"Jared invited me."

Travis glared down at me. "Sounds like something you'd do, Slocombe. You and the Professor make a real pair. Did you bring your dictionary too?"

"You jumping from there?" Abe questioned Travis.

Travis glowered down without answering.

"Will you hit the bottom?"

Travis frowned and leaped out, sailing down into the dark waters where he sliced through the surface and disappeared. A moment later his head bobbed into sight. “Why don’t you try it, Professor?” he asked as he dragged himself out on the bank.

“Back in Philly they’ve got some high dives that are three or four times that high.”

“There’s another ledge up there,” Travis commented, nodding toward the north wall. “About ten or twelve feet higher than where I was standing. Probably nothing as high as what they’ve got in Philly. Why don’t you try it, Professor?”

“I think I could.” He grinned.

“It’s pretty high,” I warned from the water. “Nobody jumps from up there very often.”

“I’m used to jumping from some pretty high places,” he came back.

I glanced up at the ledge and then back at Abe, thinking of the boasts he had made about his boxing skill. I wasn’t going to stand in his way, though.

Abe waded out to where the water was deep and then began to swim, doing a backstroke. He swam to the middle of the pond and dragged himself onto a concrete slab, which was part of the bridge. “How deep is it?” he asked, shaking water from his hair and surveying the pond.

“Find out for yourself, Professor,” Travis answered, smiling. “Get up there and jump.”

Abe looked around. All eyes were on him. Finally his gaze rested on me. “Have you done it?”

“A few times. It’s pretty high.”

"Come on, Professor," Wesley hooted. "After jumping off all those high dives in Philly, this'll be nothing."

Abe looked upward. The second ledge was nearly twenty-five feet above the pond. "Do you dive or go feet first?" Abe asked, eyeing the distance from the ledge to the pond.

Travis laughed. "Dive," he lied, shrugging. "How else?"

"Nobody's dived from up there," I came back. "Jumping is all you've got to do."

"Ah, Slocombe, why didn't you keep your mouth shut? I would have liked to have seen him dive. Like they do back in Philly."

Abe thought a moment. "How do you get up there?"

"There's a pretty decent trail to the first overhang," Travis said, pointing. "You just climb up the face of the rock to the second one. You have to take your shoes. You can't go up barefoot to the second one."

Slowly Abe climbed from the water, slipped on his ragged tennis shoes, and swam across the pond to the north wall. The climb was easy to the first overhang because there was a natural seam that jutted out and made a steep, rough trail from the pond's edge to the first ledge. Abe made it there in half a minute. He peeked over the edge and down into the water.

"Come on, Professor," Travis called out, "you're halfway there. Don't stop now."

Abe backed away from the ledge and started up the last fifteen feet to the second overhang. Slowly he inched his way up the gray, cracked granite wall, cautiously groping for fingerholds and toeholds to pull himself up. A moment later Abe was dragging himself onto the overhang. For a minute he sat on the edge, catching his breath and studying the narrow pond below. "It looks a lot higher from up here," he said, pushing himself to his feet. He touched the wall of rock behind him to steady himself.

"You're not chicken, are you?" Travis challenged.

Abe wet his lips. "You sure you don't hit the bottom?" He looked down at me.

I shook my head. "It's plenty deep. But you've got to land just right."

All eyes were on Abe. He stood up there for a long time, contemplating the plunge. Then he grinned and leaned back against the wall, shaking his head. "I'll wait until someone else does it."

"Jump, Professor," Travis ordered. "Prove you're a man."

Abe shook his head. "I'm not ready."

"Maybe he needs his glasses," Wesley called out, seeing Abe's glasses on the rock and picking them up.

He put them on the end of his nose and squinted up at Abe. "Come on, Professor. Can't you see the water from up there? Do you want me to take your glasses up to you?"

Travis and Trevor laughed. Travis stepped over to Wesley and slipped the glasses off his nose. He held them above his head and shouted up to Abe, "You can jump or you can spend the rest of the day diving for your glasses. I'm going to toss them into the pond if you don't jump, Professor."

"He said he doesn't want to jump," I spoke up. "Nobody made *you* jump."

"I've jumped from there."

"When you were ready. Not the first time you climbed up, though."

"Go drown yourself, Slocombe. The Professor's the one that said he's jumped from high dives all the time in Philly. We just want to see what he can do here." Turning back to Abe, he called out, "What's it going to be?"

Abe considered a moment and then gingerly inched again toward the edge. He wet his lips and nodded. "Set my glasses down, then."

"You jump, and then I'll set your glasses down."

For a long time Abe stood perched on the edge of the overhang and then without warning he made a short, sudden leap and sailed out into the air and began flying downward, his face contorted in a twisted grimace.

He was leaning too far backward, so instead of slicing neatly into the water, his rear and his shoulder blades slapped the surface loudly. I had a deep-down sick feeling as Abe's skinny body disappeared from sight. The water churned into white, wavy foam at the impact, and then there was nothing but the splashing of the waves along the bank and a few lingering bubbles where Abe had vanished.

All of us were standing now, staring mutely into the dark water. There was a flash of white and finally Abe's head pierced the surface. He spit, sputtered, and gasped for breath before finally exclaiming with a laugh, "Hey, I did it! It was kind of a lousy landing, but I made it down."

Some of the others were grinning and shaking their heads. I looked over at Travis and Wesley. Both were somber.

Abe swam to the bridge, dragged himself from the water, and dropped onto a flat slab of concrete.

"What did you think, Professor?" Travis asked.

"It isn't too bad, once you start down. In Philly they've got pools lots bigger and deeper than this. This is nothing to what they've got back there."

"There's one thing they don't have in Philly," Travis said. Abe looked across the pond at him. "They don't have the Cave. Why don't you shoot the Cave?"

The gaps and cracks in the rock and concrete that had tumbled into the pond to form the bridge allowed the water to wash from the upper to the lower pond. None of these cracks and holes was large enough for a person to go through except one at the very bottom of the bridge where a huge slab of concrete had fallen against a giant boulder, forming a black, narrow passageway. That was the Cave. Down there in the black, eerie bottom of the pond was where Frank Anderson had drowned, trying to swim from the upper pond to the lower. Every one of us had been warned a hundred times to stay out of the Cave. Some of us had dived down to the black entrance and explored momentarily with groping hands, but none of us had ventured inside.

"How does a guy shoot the Cave?" Abe asked calmly.

Travis grinned. "It's nothing much. At the bottom of that," he began, pointing to the rock and concrete dividing the upper and lower pond, "is a tunnel. You just swim through it to the other side. That's shooting the Cave."

"How big's the tunnel?"

"Big enough to squeeze through."

"How far down?"

"Twelve feet. Maybe a little more."

"How long is the tunnel?"

"About ten feet."

Abe studied the surface of the water as though he were looking down into the very depths of the pond and seeing the tunnel. He had stopped smiling.

"You're not chicken, are you, Professor? After all, you've had a lot of practice jumping off all those high dives back in Philly. A little pond like this wouldn't be anything to you."

Abe shook his head.

"Maybe I ought to take his glasses down to the Cave," Wesley laughed. "Maybe he'd go down then."

"Leave him alone," I spoke up. "He jumped from the ledge."

"We want to see him shoot the Cave," Travis grinned. "Why don't you back off, Slocombe?" he turned on me fiercely. "You're the one that dragged the Professor up here in the first place. If he wasn't big enough to play, you should have left him home."

"Give him his glasses," I ordered.

"Come and get them, Slocombe."

I hesitated, looking first at Travis and Wesley and then back at Abe. Slowly I turned away, feeling everybody's eyes on me.

"I knew you were yellow, Professor," Travis said. "You better stick with your books."

"Have any of you done it?" Abe asked.

"It's been done, Professor. How do you think we know it's there?" Travis asked.

Abe stared, rubbing the palms of his hands along

his wet thighs. He studied the pond a moment and then pushed himself to his feet. "Where is it?" he asked.

"Right below you and about a half dozen feet to your right. You can't miss it."

Abe took a deep breath of air and dived into the pond's dark waters.

"What if he drowns?" Chris asked me.

"How's he going to drown if he doesn't go through it?" Travis laughed.

"Maybe that's what they said about Frank Anderson," I snapped. Travis and Wesley laughed. The rest of us waited quietly and anxiously.

Suddenly Abe's head burst through the water. He was blowing and sucking in air. He wiped the water from his face and announced, "I think I found it."

"Sure you did," Wesley responded. "You just stayed down there and held your breath."

"I found an opening."

"Right," Wesley laughed, waving Abe away. "And you made it all the way through and then just turned around and came back."

"Let's get out of here," Travis suddenly called out. "We'll leave Slocombe and the Professor here together. They can shoot the Cave all day long." He started for the bushes where he had left his clothes. Wesley and Trevor followed him.

"Why don't one of you guys try it?" Abe asked.

He was still breathing heavily, and his mouth hung open as he pulled himself from the water.

Travis stopped and turned, but he didn't answer.

"You're not chicken, are you?"

Travis glared angrily at Abe. "There's a lot of things you can call me, Professor. Chicken isn't one of them."

"But you're afraid to do it, aren't you?" Abe came back.

"How would you like me to rearrange your face, Professor?"

Abe didn't answer. Travis glared at him for a long time. "Don't push your luck, Professor," he growled, "because it'd just be you and me." He nodded his head in my direction. "Don't count on Slocombe jumping in to save you." He grinned and then grabbed his clothes to get dressed.

I walked over to where Abe was sitting in the sun with his forearms on his knees and his eyes staring unseeing into the water of Baker Pond.

"Frank Anderson drowned down there, shooting the Cave," I said.

"Why didn't you tell me that before?"

"I didn't think you'd jump in."

Abe pushed himself to his feet.

"I think Frank Anderson's ghost is still around here. Sometimes this whole canyon is spooky," I said.

"I don't believe in any of that stuff," Abe responded.

"Frank Anderson didn't believe in it, either. He laughed about Jake Baker and the others. But he wasn't laughing the morning they pulled him out of the pond."

"He probably didn't know how to swim."

"He knew. Nobody in town could swim as well as Frank Anderson."

"You think he drowned because this canyon's haunted?" Abe shook his head. "They don't leave men in mines. Even dead men they dig out."

"Maybe they do in Pennsylvania. But Horace Baker didn't. He had something to hide."

"You don't know anything, Jared Slocombe," he burst out. "You don't know about mines or ghosts or anything else." Suddenly he was on his feet, stomping into the bushes. He pulled on his clothes and started down the mountain.

"He's weird, isn't he?" Chris said to me.

I nodded.

"Why'd you invite him?"

I shrugged. "He just wanted to come."

I looked around. Chris and the others were standing there, staring. Without answering, I started into the bushes for my clothes. I heard someone mumble, "We were having fun until Travis showed. I wish someone would make him take a walk."

“You volunteering?”

“I’m just saying what I think. He always ruins everything.”

Chapter 6

"Hurry, Jared," Mom called to me the next morning as I tromped in from straining the milk and putting it in the fridge on the back porch. "We can't be late for church."

"I wish we didn't have to milk on Sunday," I grumbled. "We don't do any other work. Why do we have to milk?"

"Jared," Mom cautioned, "you know those cows need milking every day."

I washed hurriedly and squeezed into my black suit, which was too short in the legs, too snug in the waist, and too much like a straight-jacket about my shoulders.

"Mom, I can't wear this suit much longer," I complained as I stepped into the bathroom where Mom was combing Megan's hair. "I'm busting out all over."

"Dad promised you a new suit when you turn twelve."

"But I don't know if I can stay inside this one that long."

"We don't have time to worry about that now, Jared. We're going to be late."

"Come on, slowpoke," Megan beamed up at me in her white Sunday dress and shiny black shoes with her long brown hair curled and combed. I was always amazed that with a little patience and work Mom could change Megan from a ponytailed tomboy into a little lady on Sunday.

"Come on, kid," I said to Megan, playfully flipping one of her curls and taking her by the hand. "Me and Meg will go save us a bench," I called over my shoulder to Mom, who was working on Michelle and Lauren.

"I wish you'd taken me swimming yesterday," Megan remarked, pouting as she clomped down the front steps and started for the gravel lane to the road. Megan didn't forget anything very easily.

"You're going to be reminding me of that for the next six months?" I grumbled.

"You could've taken me."

"You didn't miss much," I muttered.

"I could've watched."

"Some other time, Meg. When there aren't a hundred guys around for you to pester."

It was beautiful that morning as we walked down the lane listening to our Sunday shoes crunch the gravel beneath our feet. The leaves of the poplar trees along the lane rustled and whispered quietly as a gentle breeze breathed through their branches.

I always like walking the two and a half blocks to church Sunday morning along the quiet, peaceful streets of Baker's Bend. Spring was warm and in full swing. The huge sycamore trees along Miner Street had long since burst into a rich green. Birds were singing, butterflies were fluttering about, and a dog barked excitedly.

"Hey, where are you two off to?" a voice called down to us as we passed under a huge sycamore tree.

I stopped and looked up. Perched halfway up the tree, Abe straddled a limb and waved down at us. "Where you headed all dressed up?" he asked.

Megan scrunched her nose and answered boldly, "We're going to church. It's Sunday. Why aren't you going?"

"I don't go to church. Not any more."

"Why not? Are you wicked?"

Abe just shrugged. "No one cares if I go to church."

"Don't Jews go to church?" Megan pressed.

"I'm not a Jew."

"He's a Mormon, Meg," I explained in a whisper.

"You're a Mormon?" Megan gasped. "Well, then you're supposed to go to church with us. If you don't, then I guess you're just one of those wicked boys my teacher talks about."

"Maybe so." Abe shook his head forlornly.

"If you were dressed up, you could come with us, but we've got to hurry." Megan tugged on my hand. "Let's go, Jared."

I stared up in the tree at Abe. I didn't want to, but I felt a little sorry for him, sitting up there all alone on a Sunday morning. "Do you want to come with us?" I asked.

"I'm not dressed. You wouldn't want to wait for me."

"You be dressed the next time," Megan called up to him while she pulled on my hand. "We've got to get going now so we can save a seat for Mom and Michelle and Lauren. We'll save one for you too," she shouted up at Abe.

He shook his head and waved. "I don't go to church any more."

"Are we going by Loco Leo's house?" Megan asked a few minutes later, squeezing my hand. I glanced toward the old Mansion. Loco Leo was wearing bib overalls and a T-shirt and leaning against a wooden pillar on his front porch. "You won't let that crazy man get me, will you?" she whispered.

"Come on," I growled, hoarsely. "There's nothing to be afraid of."

"He's staring at us," Megan reported, unable to tear her eyes from Leo.

I reached down and turned Megan's face away

from the Mansion, pointing her gaze down the street.
"Don't stare, Meg," I warned. "He doesn't like anybody staring at him."

"How will we know if he's coming after us?"

I glanced back over my shoulder toward Leo, who was still standing on his porch with his eyes following us down the street. "He's not coming, Meg. Don't worry."

"I'm not afraid, Jared," Megan piped up. "Not with you here." She squeezed my hand and smiled up at me with her brown curls bouncing as she walked. "You're not afraid of anybody, are you? Not even Loco Leo."

I shrugged, coughing a bit. "You don't have to worry, Meg. Just forget about Leo."

"Is that crazy boy your friend?" Megan asked unexpectedly.

"What crazy boy?"

"The one in the tree."

"Abe?"

She nodded.

"I don't know him very well."

"But is he your friend?"

I thought a moment. "I guess he's okay."

"But that doesn't tell me if he's your friend."

"Well, maybe I don't know if he's my friend."

"Why isn't he your friend?"

"I didn't say that he wasn't."

"Well, is he?"

I winced. "I guess maybe he's kind of a friend."

"Then why don't you bring him to church with you? That's what you do with friends. You take them with you. You help them out. You're there when nobody else is. Didn't you know that, Jared?"

"Why do you talk so much, Meg? Besides, you're the one that said Abe was weird and crazy. Why would I take a weird, crazy guy to church with me?"

"Because he's your friend. And if somebody's your friend, it doesn't make any difference if they're crazy or weird or ugly or a lot of other things. They're just your friend and nobody has to know any more about it."

It was funny how somebody like Megan could start a guy to thinking. All through the meetings I wondered about Abe sitting up in that sycamore tree instead of sitting in church with the rest of us.

Sunday afternoon was quiet and relaxed. I was supposed to spend it at home. That was just a family rule. But this Sunday I was restless.

Mom and the girls were lying down for a nap while I tossed and turned on the living room sofa, thumbing through a book. When everything was quiet, I dropped my book, slipped out of the house through the back door, and headed down to the school. That's where a lot of the guys hung out on Sunday afternoon.

"Did you sneak out of the house?" Chris Winder

called to me with a grin from the back steps of the school. There were half a dozen guys there with him.

I blushed slightly and dropped down on the grass a few feet from the others. "I thought I'd go for a walk. What's going on?"

"We were going to play a game," Reg Ferguson said, "but there weren't enough of us."

Chris chewed a blade of grass. "Did you bring your friend?"

"My friend?"

"The Professor."

The guys laughed, and I could feel my cheeks burn red.

"Who said he was my friend? He just hangs around sometimes."

"He's a little weird, isn't he?" Reg asked.

I shrugged.

"I saw the Professor over at Loco Leo's place the other day," Chris remarked.

All of us looked at Chris.

"What was he doing there?" Reg asked.

Chris shrugged. "Beats me. They were just talking, sitting in Loco Leo's truck."

"He was talking with Loco Leo?" Skip Manning was incredulous.

Chris nodded.

"Why would anybody talk to Loco Leo?" Skip wondered.

Everyone turned to me as though I knew the answer. "What are you staring at me for? How should I know why he hangs around Loco Leo?"

"He's got to be crazy to hang around Loco Leo," Chris remarked, standing up and walking down the steps onto the grass. "A guy would have to be crazy to hang around an ex-con like Loco Leo." He laughed. "Maybe Loco Leo's his uncle."

"I'd never talk to Loco Leo," Skip muttered, running his fingers through his mop of thick red hair. "Dad says he should still be in prison for killing that guy."

"Hey, what's happening?" someone called out. We all turned around and saw Travis and Wesley coming across the grass toward us. Suddenly I wished I were home on the living room sofa. I wouldn't have left the house had I known I was going to run in to Travis and Wesley.

"We're just talking about Loco Leo and the Professor," Skip spoke up. "Chris said he saw the Professor over with Loco Leo. He said the Professor was talking to Leo like he was his uncle."

"The Professor's dumb enough for Loco Leo to be his uncle," Travis commented. "That old guy gives me the creeps. And the Professor's not much better."

"Hey, there's a dead cat down on the highway," Wesley announced. "Just killed. We ought to take it over to Loco Leo's and hang it on his front porch. He loves dead dogs and cats and things." Wesley grinned mischievously.

"He'll cut your gizzard out," Reg Ferguson warned, wetting his lips.

"He won't if he doesn't catch us," Wesley countered.

"He sure got mad when we dragged that dead collie into his yard and put it in his truck behind the steering wheel," Reg said, shuddering. "He said he'd get us for that one."

"You chicken, Ferg?" Wesley asked with a grin.

Reg gulped and looked around. "I'm just not crazy." His dark eyes were wide, and his lips started to twitch nervously.

"Then you'd drag that cat up on Leo's porch, would you?"

"Old Leo won't do anything," Travis said, walking over to Reg and pulling his baseball cap off his head and dropping it into his lap. "He's usually sleeping Sunday afternoons. Most of the time he's drunk too."

"But that's when he's mean," Reg rasped, picking his cap from his lap and putting it on his head again. "He was drunk when he killed that man."

"Come on, Reg, you're not afraid to take old Loco Leo his dead cat, are you?"

I don't think there was one of us besides Travis and Wesley, and maybe Skip Manning, who really wanted to bother Loco Leo that Sunday afternoon, but none of us managed to say so. I guess each of us was waiting for someone else to protest. When no one did, we all ended up following Travis and Wesley down to the highway to look for the dead cat.

I didn't like Leo and I was afraid of him, but I didn't like doing mean things to him, either. Mom and Dad had both warned me not to bother him. I would have felt bad bothering Leo any day, but I felt especially guilty today because it was Sunday. How I wished I were still home, thumbing through the pages of a book.

I grimaced as Wesley hooked a piece of baling twine around the dead cat's neck and picked it up.

With Wesley lugging the dead, mangled cat, all of us headed toward Leo's place. We stopped across the street from the old Mansion and hid behind a clump of wild rose bushes that grew in an empty lot there. We studied the place for a few minutes, looking for any sign of Leo.

The Mansion was three stories high with pointed, gabled windows, most of them boarded up. The roof was pocked by patches of bare boards where the shingles had long since blown away. At one time the Mansion must have been white, but winter cold and summer sun had peeled most of the paint away.

Running the entire width of the house was a sagging front porch, partially supported by wooden pillars. Many of the floor boards were broken and cracked. Huge sycamore and oak trees crowded the front yard, which was infested with weeds and overrun by Virginia creeper and rose bushes.

Even looking at the old Mansion in the daylight gave me the creeps. I shuddered at the thought of ever entering that evil place and coming face to face with the crazy man who lived there.

"Hey, Slocombe," Travis whispered, "you go with Reg. It's your turn."

My head jerked around. Travis took the dead cat from Wesley and held it out to me.

"But I don't—" I started to protest. The words caught in my throat.

"You promised the last time," Travis said. "When we put the dog in his truck, you wanted to be the lookout, but you said you'd go for sure the next time."

I glanced over at Reg, who had a sick look on his face.

"You're not chicken, are you?" Wesley taunted.

"I ain't chicken of nothing," I lied, "but I don't like messing around Leo's place, either."

"He's chicken, all right," Travis sneered. "Just like his friend the Professor."

I hesitated a moment. Reaching for the dead cat while two fat flies buzzed about the crushed head, I felt a rumbling in the pit of my stomach. "Come on," I rasped over my shoulder at Reg.

I knew if I hesitated, even a moment, I would lose

courage and never go, and I knew the taunting and teasing that would follow if I backed down.

Reg and I dashed across the street and ducked behind a rose bush crawling with clinging Virginia creeper. We waited there a moment to catch our breath and then made one last dash up the front steps and onto the porch that creaked and moaned under our weight. A broken board sagged down from the porch ceiling and I reached up and looped the baling twine around it. Leaving the dangling dead cat, the two of us leaped from the porch, but as we did we heard the front door bang open. "Hey, there!" a hoarse voice crackled behind us.

I glanced over my shoulder and there stood Leo in the door way with his infamous walking stick in one hand while he held his other hand in a tightly clenched fist and shook it at us above his head. "You'll pay for this, boy. I know you. You live just down the street in the yellow house. I know where to find you."

I was running now, faster than I had ever run before. The others, who were waiting across the street, scattered. I didn't know where Reg was. I didn't care. The only thing that mattered was to get as far from Leo and his haunted house as I could possibly get.

I didn't stop running until I reached home. I burst into the back door and all but collapsed onto the floor. My heart was pounding in my chest, and huge gasping breaths of air burned at my throat and lungs. I looked out the door once to make sure I hadn't been followed, and then I crept down the hall to my room, where I collapsed onto the bed.

Chapter 7

It was late afternoon when I finally awoke, but I didn't leave my room. I stayed there and let the minutes tick away, tormented by the picture of Leo standing on his front porch next to the dead cat, shaking his fist at me and growling his threat.

I could hear Mom and the girls in the kitchen popping corn. Usually I would have gone out and helped, but not today. Stalling, I made my bed, straightened my room, organized my drawers, and even rearranged my desk and dresser.

It was past seven, the sun was setting, and dusk was beginning to creep across our yard when I finally wandered down the hall to the kitchen.

"Have you finished the milking?" Mom asked when she saw me.

"Not yet."

"Jared, it's past seven. You should have finished milking over an hour ago. What have you been doing?"

"I guess I fell asleep, and then I started doing

some things in my room," I mumbled scratching my head.

"Can I go with you, Jared?" Meg asked with her fist full of popcorn.

"Sure," I said, wanting the company. "Go out on the back porch and grab the bucket. I'll be down at the corral feeding the calves and the horse."

I left the porch and headed for the barn. The sun was about to sink behind the gray-blue mountains to the west, and darkness was crowding about me. I quickened my pace, not wanting to be outside milking when darkness finally fell.

"Jared," Meg called to me as I was climbing down from the hay stack, "I can't find the bucket."

"It's hanging on the back porch," I grumbled.

Meg shook her head and rubbed her nose with the palm of her hand. "I looked. I even checked in the house."

"Oh, Meg, you're blind. Go look again. This time with your eyes open."

"But, Jared, I– "

"Meg, just do it. I'll be putting the cows in the barn. We've got to hurry. It's getting late."

"Jared," Meg spoke, "why do you suppose Loco Leo was hanging around our place today?"

I whipped around and stared at her. "What makes you think he was around here?"

"I saw him, coming up the lane."

"Are you lying, Meg?"

She shook her head. "Honest."

"Where'd he go?"

She shrugged. "I don't know. I hid under the covers."

"You sure it was him?"

She nodded again. "He had his walking stick. He was carrying something else. But I don't know what it was."

"Go get the bucket, Meg," I ordered.

I looked toward the barn, and a sick feeling exploded inside me. I swallowed hard, walked to the barn door, and flung it open. I couldn't see anything, only the dark interior of the barn. Suddenly I wished I had come sooner, when there was more light.

The barn wasn't large, maybe twenty by thirty feet, but there were no windows in it, and in late evening it was almost pitch black. There was only a single light bulb with a string pull switch hanging from the rafters in the middle of the barn.

I wet my lips and crept forward, squinting into the blackness. Nervously I brushed the back of my hand across my forehead. I took two steps forward, stopped and listened. I could hear nothing. Slowly I crept forward with my hand out, groping for the light.

I was halfway across the barn floor when something damp and furry brushed across my face. I yelled and slapped at it, and the wet, furry mass knocked against my face again.

Turning, I stumbled for the door, snagging my foot on a loose board. I struggled to catch myself, but I was too wobbly and I crashed headlong into the doorway. My breath was knocked out of me, but I scrambled to my feet and lunged outside, where I stumbled and fell again.

Sitting on the ground, I stared back toward the barn, too shaken to move.

"What you doing?"

I whipped around and pushed myself to my feet in one frantic movement. Meg was standing there, staring.

"What's the matter?" she asked.

"Nothing," I mumbled, shaking my head.

Just inside the barn door was a pitchfork. I grabbed it and began creeping forward, every muscle in my body tense. This time as I crossed the floor I made a wide circle toward the light. I didn't bump into anything. I groped in the blackness for the light and pulled the string. A pale yellow light brightened up the interior. Not five feet from me, hanging from the rafters, was the dead cat I had left at Leo's place that afternoon.

"What's that doing here?" Meg asked from the doorway of the barn.

I didn't answer her. Instead I swung the pitchfork

at the dangling cat and knocked it across the barn. Grabbing the twine that was still around the cat's neck, I dragged it outside and tossed it over the fence into some weeds. Meg followed me.

"Who would hang a dead cat in our barn?" Meg demanded.

"Where's the bucket, Meg?" I snapped.

"It's not there, Jared. I looked again."

"It's got to be. I put it there this morning."

"You looking for your bucket?" Abe asked unexpectedly.

I turned. Abe was leaning against the corral fence next to the barn. "Leo took it."

"Leo? What does he want with our milk bucket?"

Abe shrugged. "I guess he figures *you* want it. I came over earlier to see what you were going to do about it. I was going to tell you about the dead cat in the barn too, but no one was stirring around here, so I just left."

I gulped, my mind racing to think of what else I might use to milk the cows. There was nothing. And I knew I couldn't talk to Mom or I would have to tell her what I had been doing on a Sunday afternoon.

"But why would he take my bucket?"

"Why would you hang a dead cat on his porch?"

"Who said I did?"

"I saw you."

"We were just having fun."

"Maybe that's what he's doing."

Meg was staring first at me and then at Abe, not understanding anything. "What's he talking about, Jared?"

"Meg, run to the house. Tell Mom I'll be up in a bit."

"But what about the bucket?"

"Meg. Please. And don't say anything to Mom or the girls."

"Where's the bucket now?" I asked when Meg was gone.

"On his front porch, next to his front door."

For a long time I stood in front of the barn, pondering. It was getting darker every minute. I had to do something quick or I would be forced to return to Leo's house in the dead of night.

"Do you want me to come along?" Abe asked calmly.

"Will you?"

"Sure."

A few minutes later we were standing across the street from the Mansion. I squinted toward the old house, and there on the front porch I spotted the shiny milk bucket, right where Abe had said it would be. For several minutes I stared, too afraid to move.

"Well, are you going to go get it?" Abe asked.

I licked my lips and glanced over at him. He was calm. "Aren't you afraid?" I questioned.

"He's just an old man."

"He's crazy, mean crazy. Only a mean crazy man would do something like this."

"Are you mean crazy because you hung that dead cat on his front porch?"

"But I didn't mean anything by it." I studied Abe. "Are you afraid?"

He shook his head.

"If you're not afraid, why don't you go get the bucket?" I challenged.

He shook his head. "I don't want him to think that I was part of anything that happened today. It's not because I think he's crazy. He's just an old man. Like a million other old men."

"You don't know him."

"*You* don't know him. What can he do to you?"

"He could drag me into his house, lock me up and torture me—even kill me."

"He wouldn't do that."

"He's been to prison for killing a man."

"If he's been to prison, then I'd guess that he doesn't ever want to go back. That's why he won't do anything to you. You might even like him if you got to know him."

"Why would I want to know him?"

Abe shrugged. "I know him. He's a friend of mine."

"A friend of yours? Why would you want a friend like that? He's crazy and weird."

Abe stared at me, puzzled. "If he's my friend, it shouldn't make any difference if some people think he's crazy or weird or a hundred other things. He's still my friend."

Leaving Abe behind, I started toward the Mansion. At first I walked slowly; then I broke into a run and sprinted across the yard under the oak and sycamore trees. I bounded up the front steps and creaked across the porch to the bucket. I grabbed for it and pulled, but it wouldn't come. In horror I looked down and saw that it was wired to the broken boards of the porch floor. Sick with fright, I dropped to my knees and began tearing frantically at the wire, jerking and tugging until I finally wrenched the bucket free. Then, with the bucket under my arm, I turned and leaped from the porch. As I did, I ran into Leo, who had been leaning on his gnarled walking stick, watching me.

The force of the impact knocked me backwards and onto the ground. The bucket clanged and rolled away from me. I wanted to leap to my feet and sprint to safety, but I was petrified. Leo took two steps, reached down, and grabbed my arm. Roughly he pulled me to my feet. The first thought that burst into my mind was that I was going to be dragged into the Mansion and killed.

"So you came back?" he growled angrily. "I knew if I waited long enough, you'd have to come for your precious bucket. Now you're mine."

"Let me go," I begged, my voice almost a sob. "Please let me go. I'll never bother you again."

"Sure," he answered. "No, you won't bother me until you get to the street. Then you'll forget your promises and start calling your names and throwing rocks. And next week you'll be back with something else."

"I won't," I pleaded, feeling tears of terror in my eyes. "I didn't want to do anything today. Honest. I won't come back. Ever."

"Leo," I heard Abe speak behind me. I craned my head around. Abe was standing there, not ten feet away. "He won't bother you any more," Abe said. "I'll make sure."

"How will you make sure?" Leo demanded.

"He's my friend."

Slowly Leo's iron grip loosened and finally released me. I crumpled to the ground. Leo didn't say any more. He turned and walked back onto his porch. It was too dark for me to see his face, but I felt his dark, squinting eyes bore into me.

Gathering strength that I didn't realize I had, I pushed myself to my feet, grabbed the bucket, and sprinted past Abe to safety. I didn't stop until I reached the barn.

A few minutes later Abe followed me in. "He didn't kill you," Abe remarked.

"Just because of you." I was still panting and shaking while my heart pounded in my chest. "Thanks," I choked. "He'd still have me if you hadn't stopped him."

Abe shrugged. "You still afraid of him?"

I didn't answer.

"If he wanted to do anything to you, he could have done it tonight. He could have waited for you in the barn. He could have dragged you into his house and tortured you. But he didn't do any of those things."

"Only because of you."

"Maybe."

"How can you stand him, Abe? How can you stand to be around him?"

"He's my friend."

"Why would you ever want a friend like him?"

He stared at me a moment and turned away, leaving me standing in the barn.

Chapter 8

Monday Abe waited for me after school. In fact, from then on he waited for me after school each day. He worked alongside me as I did my janitor work, and then we walked home together. Some afternoons he helped me with my home chores too. We didn't have a lot to do with each other at school, though. He stuck with his books or sat on the back steps of the school and watched while the rest of us played ball.

Travis and Wesley, and sometimes Trevor and Skip, made life miserable for Abe. They pestered him, hiding his books, stuffing wads of paper in his desk when he went to the pencil sharpener, and hitting him in the back of the head with spit wads when Mr. Preston had his head down at his desk.

One Friday after school all of us raced to the ball diamond. Mom had told me to get my janitor work finished early so I could hurry home and hoe some weeds before I did the milking, but Travis and Wesley had been bragging all day about how they were going to cream the bunch of us after school. I couldn't let the team down, so I decided to stay and play and answer to Mom later.

Chris Winder had left school halfway through the afternoon with a toothache, leaving our team one player short. And Chris wasn't one we could afford to lose.

"We can't play them without Chris," Brandon Perkins complained as we were sizing up our team. Brandon was the biggest kid in the sixth grade, even bigger than Wesley, but he was a lot on the chunky side and quite a whiner. "They'll smear us good," he complained, pulling up the baggy pants that hung down on his hips. "Who'll pitch?"

"You can have the Professor," Wesley joked. "He's coming out right now," he added, nodding to where Abe was slowly clomping down the back steps.

"Yeah," Travis grinned, poking Wesley with an elbow. "That will make the teams even. Just don't let him be the umpire. He's cross-eyed."

"We don't want the Professor," Brandon protested.

"What good would he be?" Reg joined in. "What's he going to do, come out here and read us one of his books?"

I hesitated a moment and swallowed before speaking up. "We'll take him," I said, trying to sound casual. Ever since the incident with Leo Lucero, I had wanted to invite Abe to play with us. I just hadn't known how until now.

A sudden chorus of no's erupted from my team.

"We need another guy." I shrugged. "Maybe he's an okay player."

"The Professor?" Reg asked doubtfully.

I nodded. "He's better than nothing."

Reg Ferguson shrugged and remarked, "Maybe he can at least fall in front of the ball and stop it."

Turning in Abe's direction, I shouted, "Hey, Abe, we're one short. Come and play."

For a moment Abe hesitated, not sure that he was really being invited. I waved again and slowly he ambled over.

"I don't have a mitt," he explained as he walked up.

Skip Manning tossed him his. "Have you ever worn one?" he teased. For a moment Abe studied the ball glove without putting it on. "No, Professor, you wear it, not read it."

Abe slipped the glove on his hand and smashed his fist into its pocket. He licked his lips and then grinned. "Just right," he declared.

"He even put it on the right hand," Skip joked and everyone laughed.

"In Philly," Abe started to speak, "I had—"

"We don't want to know what you did in Philly,"

Travis cut him short. "Let's see what you can do in Baker's Bend."

Russell Larsen usually played shortstop for us, but with Chris gone I wanted him to pitch. "Hey, Russell, why don't you pitch? Reg can play short for you, and Abe, you take right field." I wanted Abe someplace where he couldn't do much damage.

"Ah, come on, Slocombe, let the Professor take Chris's place on the mound," Travis laughed. "We'll give him some experience."

"You can play right field," I said.

"Put him in as pitcher," Wesley said. "At least for an inning. I've got a ball all ready for him. You won't be able to catch it with one of your books, though, Professor."

"He's going to play right field," I came back.

"Hey, Professor, pitch," Travis ordered. "You can lob that ball across the plate and handle a line drive or two, can't you?"

Abe grinned and brushed his long brown hair from his narrow face. "Sure. In Philly I used to pitch all the time. Our team went 17 and 2 when I pitched for them."

"You've got your pitcher, Slocombe," Travis grinned at me.

Abe smiled at me. "It's okay, Jared. I've played a lot of ball before."

"You said you were a killer with a pair of boxing gloves too."

"I *know* about boxing. But I *play* baseball."

I finally gave in, over the protests of my own team, and let Abe pitch. "This is just for one inning," I told Travis and his team. "Then Russell pitches."

"After one inning with the Professor, it won't matter who they put in as pitcher," Wesley laughed.

Skip was the first to bat for the other team. Travis and Wesley gave him a few whispered instructions, and he stepped to the plate and grinned at Abe.

"This is probably coming your way, Abe," I called out nervously. "Watch for a line drive. And don't be afraid to duck. Tim will pick it up in centerfield."

Abe casually tossed the ball into his glove a half dozen times. I was angry with myself for letting Travis and Wesley push me into allowing Abe to pitch.

Abe leaned forward toward home plate. He took a deep breath and threw the ball. There was nothing special about it, but it did make it across the plate, something I hadn't been sure Abe could even do.

Skip let the first two pitches go by, waiting for just the right one, and when it came, he met the ball solidly. There was a loud crack and the ball sailed out two or three feet above Abe's head and a little to his right. Abe leaped into the air and his left hand reached up and over and snagged the ball.

Everything happened so quickly that no one really

realized what had happened until Abe pulled the ball from his glove. Shaking and scratching his head, Skip walked back from first base and joined his teammates.

"Good catch, Abe," I laughed. "Did that one surprise you?"

"I said I'd played before."

"I'm next," Wesley announced somberly, grabbing a bat and stomping up to home plate. He glared out toward Abe. "See if you can catch this one, Professor."

"Get ready, Abe," I said. "He can really knock it."

Wesley let the first five pitches go by, waiting for just the right one.

"He's throwing strikes," I complained. "You've got to swing at them if they're good."

"I'll swing when I'm ready," Wesley growled. "I haven't seen one with the Professor's name on it yet."

The right ball came on the seventh pitch. Wesley put all his weight into it, and it fired out toward the field like a bullet, straight for Abe's head. It was the kind of hit that you want to get out of the way of, but Abe didn't jump away. In one smooth motion he snatched the ball from the air. The force of the impact knocked him off balance, and he fell to the grass. But he didn't lose the ball.

"I don't believe it," Travis muttered. "Two lucky catches, just like that."

Abe shook his head. "No, I played ball in Philly."

"We don't want to hear any more about Philly. I'm batting."

Abe took his time and sent the ball flying across homeplate, this time with some real zing on it. Travis swung. And missed completely. Our team cheered.

"Don't celebrate yet," Travis warned.

He let the next two pitches pass him, although they were clear strikes. But they were fast. I could see now that Abe had played some ball before. On the next pitch Travis swung again and got just a small piece of the ball, popping it up behind him.

Abe got ready for the next pitch. Holding the ball behind him, he looked intently toward home plate and then he wound up for the pitch. It looked like he was going to throw that ball clear into next week. Travis stiffened and braced himself for the pitch, but when Abe let the ball fly it wasn't a fast one. In fact, it wasn't much more than a lob. But it was too late for Travis. He was already swinging so hard that he spun clear around before Abe's pitch even reached home plate. I had never seen Travis Williams strike out. And there was no way that he could cheat and change the call!

It was a mean game with lots of complaining and arguing and name calling, but we won by two runs. Travis got one base hit and popped out twice to left field. He had never played a worse game.

"Looks like we've got a pitcher," Brandon grinned as we all gathered at the end of the game. "The Professor can do a lot more than just read."

"Were you really 17 and 2 back in Philly?" Reg questioned.

Abe grinned and nodded.

"You played all right," I complimented him as we walked into the school so I could do my janitor work.

He smiled. "I told you I'd played before."

"You could make the team in Fairview this summer."

Abe shook his head. "I don't know if I'll be here this summer."

I stopped. "Well, where would you be?"

He shrugged. "That's just it. I don't know. If Aunt Ruth doesn't think she can keep me – " He hesitated and looked down. "What do orphans do?" he asked sadly.

"Orphan?" I asked. "You're not an orphan."

"I'm not?" he asked, looking up.

"I thought orphans were just in books and movies."

"Both my mom and dad are dead. My brother's dead. None of my relatives want me, unless Aunt Ruth and Uncle Reuben want to keep me."

"Are you afraid?"

He thought a moment and then nodded his head. "I guess a little. I'm afraid to be alone."

"I didn't think you cared. I mean, you always go off by yourself. I just kind of figured that you didn't mind it that way."

"Nobody likes it that way. Sometimes I've got to do it, but I don't like it. In Philly I wasn't ever alone. Not until Mom died." He looked over at me. "You're scared of crazy things, like the ghosts up in the old mine, something you can't even see. I guess I'm a little like that. I'm scared of what I can't see. Not ghosts, though. I am scared about what's going to happen to me. I figure that's why I don't like to be alone."

"Is that why you hang around Loco Leo, so you won't be alone?"

"Leo's alone too. Together we're not alone any more. I'm not so scared when I'm around him."

"I'd be scared to be around him. I think I'd rather be alone."

"It's easy for you to say that because you've never been alone." He looked at me. "Thanks for letting me play today, Jared." He smiled. "I liked it. I liked it a lot. Do you think I can do it again?"

I grinned. "Why not? We need a good pitcher."

Chapter 9

The next day I took Abe to the pond again. Most of the guys were there. Nobody complained about Abe's being there, but I could tell that Travis was still upset about yesterday's game. Everybody else seemed to have forgotten it.

Abe jumped from the overhang again. In fact, he jumped a dozen times, until he became pretty sure of himself. At least, he didn't tense up and fall backwards, almost breaking his back like he had done the first day.

The morning passed quickly, and afternoon blazed hot. Eventually all of us found cover in the shade and lay on the new spring grass, gazing up into the rustling branches of the maple trees.

"You know what we ought to do this afternoon?" Travis mused. We waited. He grabbed his pants from under a nearby bush and felt in the pockets. He pulled out a small yellow flashlight. "We ought to give the Professor a tour of the mine," he said, holding up the flashlight.

Everyone's gaze went to Travis and then slowly shifted to Abe, who sat on the edge of the group poking at the ground with a stick. "What do you say, Professor?"

Abe looked up at Travis. "I've seen mines before," he answered with a shrug of his shoulders. "They have lots of them in Pennsylvania. They're no big deal."

Travis pulled the corners of his mouth down, clicked the light on and off, and then stuffed it back into his pants pocket. Snatching a stick in front of him, he broke it and tossed the two pieces into the bushes. "The Baker Mine isn't like anything you've got in Pennsylvania." He studied Abe. "Old Jake Baker's ghost wanders around in the mines."

"I don't believe in ghosts." Abe grinned, but the grin was forced.

"You wouldn't be afraid to go in the mine, then?"

Abe's grin drooped, and he swallowed. "I'm not afraid of ghosts."

Travis looked over at Wesley and laughed. "The Professor's not afraid of anything." Wesley smiled and looked at Abe. "You've never met Jake Baker," Travis added.

"We're not supposed to go up there," Reg spoke up. "Something always happens when somebody goes up there."

"You don't have to go, Ferg. I *know* you're chicken."

"It's crazy to go in there," Reg added. "Some of the scouts started poking around in the mine last summer. I know. My brother was one of them. The tunnel started to cave in." Reg shook his head. "Dad says there are places in the mine where there isn't any air. You could get caught back there and suffocate. Dad told me he'd give me a lickin' I'd never forget if I even went up around the mines."

"Well, Reggie boy," Travis mocked, "we don't want your daddy to give you a lickin'. Why don't you grab your things and toddle on down the mountain to your mommy and daddy."

Reg stood up and grabbed his clothes. He stared down at Travis. "It doesn't have anything to do with being scared. It's stupid to go up there."

"The Professor here isn't afraid of anything," Travis shrugged as Reg started down the trail, followed by Brandon and Chris and several others. "They're all chicken," Travis muttered.

"I said I wasn't afraid of ghosts. That's all I said."

"You just don't want to go up to the Baker Mine, is that it?"

Abe dropped his stick and stood up. "I've seen plenty of mines. I could look at this one," he announced.

"You don't have to do it, Abe," I spoke up.

"Slocombe, the Professor *wants* to do it. You can

go home with Reg." Travis started into the bushes for his clothes.

Wesley and Skip Manning pushed themselves to their feet. Slowly, one by one, the rest of us stood and started getting dressed. The others headed down the mountain as soon as they had their clothes on. Only Travis, Wesley, Skip, Abe, and I remained.

"Come on, Abe," I said, "we don't have to go up there."

"Slocombe, let him make up his own mind."

"I'm not afraid of the ghosts, Jared," Abe said quietly, avoiding my eyes.

"You ready, Professor?" Travis asked.

"My dad and uncle worked in a mine," Abe commented lightly.

"They didn't work in the Baker Mine. If they had, they'd be buried up there right now with Jake Baker and his friends. They'd be ghosts too."

"Nobody's buried there," Abe came back seriously. "They would have dug them out a long time ago."

"Horace Baker didn't want to dig them out," Travis said

"It's true," Wesley spoke for the first time. "When the mine caved in, nobody dared dig them out because they figured the whole mountain would come down on them, leaving them back there screaming and begging too."

"I don't believe that," Abe repeated simply, shaking his head.

"It's true," Skip spoke out. "My grandpa saw Jake's wolf dog with his own eyes. That was five years after the mine caved in on top of Jake and his dog. And my grandpa ain't a liar. And he wasn't just trying to spook me. He saw the wolf dog. Lots of people have seen his tracks. Two of the dog's toes were cut off on his front left paw. There was no mistaking his track. And people have seen those tracks."

"How'd your grandpa see that dog if the dog got buried?" Abe demanded.

"It was his ghost."

"A ghost doesn't leave tracks."

"This one does."

"Maybe the dog didn't die."

"Old Jake Baker didn't go anyplace without his dog," Skip insisted. "People saw Jake go into the mine with his dog the day the mine caved in. Nobody saw them leave. My dad says if you go back in the mine, to where the tunnel is closed off from the cave-in, you can hear the screams of those buried miners."

"I went into the mine with my uncle," Travis said without smiling. "Back to the fork in the tunnel. The right tunnel is closed off from the cave-in. I heard those screams."

"They don't leave dead men in mines," Abe burst out, shaking his head furiously. He seemed worried.

I could tell by the way his hands twitched and his Adam's apple bobbed when he swallowed.

"Do you have the guts to go up and see for yourself?"

I was hoping Abe would refuse. Every one of us, including Travis, wanted Abe to play the coward and keep us from the Baker Mine.

"I'll go," Abe announced. "With the rest of you," he added.

"You think we're chicken?" Travis bristled. Abe didn't answer. Travis stepped toward Abe, glaring at him. "Let's show the Professor the Baker Mine."

We didn't laugh and joke as we climbed. If we talked at all, it was just above a whisper.

A rocky, winding trail led to the mines at the top of Baker Canyon. It criss-crossed back and forth across the rugged canyon as it worked its way up the steep incline. The trail was overgrown with bushes and trees, but in most places it was still easy enough to follow.

At the bottom of the canyon, birds sang, squirrels chattered, and bugs buzzed, but as we climbed higher and drew nearer to the mine itself, a hush seemed to fall over everything, and chilling goose bumps sprouted on the back of my neck.

We hiked for nearly forty-five minutes up the steep incline. A huge wall of gray granite that jutted upward a hundred feet almost completely blocked off the upper end of the canyon. It seemed to challenge our very presence on the mountain. But we pressed forward, following the mule trail that led to a narrow passage between the canyon wall and the jagged wall of granite. That passageway was the only entrance into the upper canyon.

As we stepped from the passage, the upper part of Baker Canyon stretched before us. It was a small valley of sorts, filled with tall pine trees and thick, tangled brush. In the bottom of this valley were several log structures, crumbling with decay. The roofs of all of them had long since fallen in or been blown away. There was one large two-story building. The upper story was almost gone, but the lower story was still pretty much intact.

"That's where the miners stayed," Skip remarked, pointing down to the rotting buildings. "The big one is where Horace Baker stayed when he was around."

"They look spooky," Wesley spoke, gulping and chewing on his lower lip.

"Those must be the mines," Abe spoke up.

We all turned around and stared at Abe. He was behind us, pointing to the north wall of the canyon. We looked in the direction he was pointing. Several long yellow ore slides stained the green mountainside.

"The mines are above those, aren't they?" He ran his tongue along his upper lip and then pressed his lips together.

Skip, who seemed to know as much as anyone about the mines, spoke. "The main one is the one farthest east. It goes almost a half mile back into the mountain. At least it did before it caved in. That's where everybody's buried."

We all studied the side of the canyon, focusing on the largest ore slide.

"It sure is quiet up here," Wesley commented, looking about the upper canyon.

"What do you think, Professor?" Travis asked.

Abe had paled some, but he started forward without answering. When he was thirty feet or so in front of us, he stopped and turned around. None of us had moved. He studied us for a moment. "You coming?" he asked, his voice cracking.

Travis took a deep breath. "Come on," he grumbled. "Let's give the Professor his tour."

On our way to the north wall and the main mine we passed the abandoned cabins and glanced inside their gray, rotting pine skeletons with the windows gone and doors torn away.

"That's where they loaded the ore," Skip spoke up, pointing to a huge structure made of giant timbers and connected to a stretch of rusted, twisted tracks. "They loaded the ore in metal buckets hanging on a huge cable and hauled it down the mountain to the pond. Big ore wagons pulled by mule teams carried it to Baker's Bend for the railroad."

Slowly we climbed the yellow ore slide. Abe was the first to reach the top. As I scrambled up next to him, I saw the crumbling wooden structure at the mouth of the mine. It looked like a small house with the front wall missing. The boards and timbers were gray from years of weather. I looked into the dim shadows of the structure and saw the black, gaping hole of the mine itself.

"There it is," Travis declared.

"But you can't prove that anybody's buried back there." Abe declared, staring nervously at the mine entrance. "Even if we went back, we couldn't prove anything."

"It goes back about a quarter mile," Skip spoke. "Then it splits. The left fork goes back another couple hundred yards. The right fork is what caved in. That's where Jake Baker and his friends are buried. Before the cave-in, that part went back another quarter mile. If you stand there by the cave-in and listen, you can hear the groans and screams of those men. That's how you know they're there."

Abe took several steps forward and entered the crumbling structure at the entrance of the mine. He looked about, examining everything. Turning from it, he faced the rest of us. "It's not smart to go in old mines." Nervously he wiped his mouth with the back of his hand.

Travis reached into his back pocket and pulled out

his disposable flashlight. "Let's go, Professor," he said solemnly, starting forward. Abe didn't answer. Travis stepped into the mine and turned around. "Come on," he commanded the rest of us. "You aren't chicken too, are you?"

I think if any one of us had backed down, Travis would have given up his crazy notion of entering the mine. But no one protested. Wesley moved forward, followed by Skip Manning. I was next. Abe stared at us, wearing fear like a gray mask. He stared first at Travis and then at me. Our eyes locked for just a moment before I looked away.

Slowly Abe followed, and as he did fear gripped me like a cold monstrous claw. Travis's light flicked on, and the blackness of the cave swallowed us, leaving us alone with the bobbing yellow ray from the tiny flashlight.

Our husky breathing and the trample of our shuffling feet echoed dully from the damp, jagged walls of the cave. Occasionally we came to places where pieces of rock and dirt had broken away overhead and crumbled to the mine floor. Huge timbers were spaced along the walls and overhead to support the mountain above us. Some of them were bowed and cracked. Others were tilted at awkward angles.

I'm not sure how far we walked. It seemed forever, but it was probably less than two hundred yards. The entrance to the mine was only a bright spot behind us.

"This is crazy!" Abe suddenly burst out. "We could all be buried alive. Look at those walls. Look at the ceiling. Everything is ready to fall in."

"And no one would find us," Travis said, trying hard not to reveal his own fears. "We'd be buried alive. And nobody would come and get us. Nobody. But we'd have company in here."

"They don't leave people buried in mines," Abe burst out, walking away from us, stumbling and falling toward the light at the mouth of the mine. The rest of us stood still, seeing his departing silhouette and hearing his unsteady steps. And all of us wished we were with him.

"Let's get out of here," Wesley whined. "The Professor's right. We could get killed in here."

"Shut up!" Travis snapped. He attempted a laugh, but it was only a shaky grunt. "We'll stay here a while," he whispered, flashing the light about. "We'll tell the Professor we went all the way to the cave-in." Suddenly he flicked the light off. The rest of us gasped, reaching for each other.

"Come on, Travis," Wesley whispered in a shaky voice. "This isn't funny. Turn that light back on."

"Well, I don't know about you guys, but I'm going back," I said. "You can pretend to be brave all you want."

"Shut up, Slocombe," growled Travis. He flicked the flashlight on again. "You explore mines just like you play baseball. You're as bad as the Professor."

I didn't answer him but turned and picked my way back to the mine entrance, stumbling over the debris on the floor. I heard the others following close behind.

When we finally stepped into daylight again, I thought I had never been so glad to see the sun and to breathe real air.

Abe sat on a rotting pine log with his forearms on his bony knees, staring at us as we filed from the mine.

"Well, we made it, Professor," Travis announced.

"They're buried in there for sure," Wesley said. "We heard their screams."

Abe looked away, studying the mountain that loomed above us.

Suddenly Travis called out, "Professor," and tossed his flashlight toward Abe. Although Abe was off guard, he caught the flashlight and gripped it tightly in his hands. "It's your turn, Professor."

Abe stared wide-eyed at Travis without speaking or moving.

"If you're going to hang around us, you're going to have to go in there." He nodded back toward the mine. "Like the rest of us did. We don't hang around with chickens."

Abe was motionless.

"Don't swim with us," Travis went on. "Don't play

ball with us. Don't talk to us. Don't even look at us. You'll always be all alone."

For the longest time Abe didn't move while we all waited. Then slowly he pushed himself to his feet. He wet his lips and dug his fists deep into his pockets. "Nobody leaves dead men in mines," he declared.

"Tell us that when you come back," Travis answered. "If you come back." He laughed. "We made a pile of rocks by the cave-in and one more at the very back of the left tunnel. Go back and tell us how many rocks are in each pile. Then we'll know you made it all the way."

Abe looked at me. I couldn't look away, and yet I couldn't speak. He was like a guy drowning and reaching for someone to rescue him. But I let him drown. He turned and started down the mountain.

"Aren't you going in, Professor? You said you weren't scared of ghosts," Travis taunted.

"They don't leave men in mines," he shouted back. And then he started to run. I started after him. I caught up to him just above the pond.

"You all right, Abe?" I asked, panting to catch my breath.

"Leave me alone," he muttered over his shoulder.

"We didn't go to the back. We stopped right where you left us. We didn't take another step. And we didn't hear anything."

He looked at me. "Why didn't you say that up there?"

I shrugged. "I don't know. I guess I was scared."

"Of Travis?"

I shook my head. "I'm not afraid of Travis," I burst out. "I was just – " I groped for an explanation. "I was still nervous about the mine."

"Leave me alone."

"You don't have to believe all that junk that Travis said about you being alone and not able to hang around the rest of us. He can't do that to you. Not if we don't want him to."

"Leave me alone, Jared."

"I want to help you, Abe."

"Why? Because nobody's around now? That's the only time you ever want to help. When nobody's around to see. You're even worse than they are. At least Travis doesn't ever pretend to like me."

His sudden accusation was like a sharp slap across my face. I stopped on the trail and watched him disappear down the mountain.

Chapter 10

I didn't see Abe until Monday morning when he quietly took his place across the aisle from me.

"We're going to play a short game after school," I ventured uneasily. "Come play with us." The whole weekend I had wanted to make up for Saturday afternoon at the mine. I coughed. "You'll play, won't you?"

He stared at his books without speaking.

I glanced up at Mr. Preston, who was writing on the board. "You can play with our team," I whispered. "I'm sorry about the other day."

That afternoon I hurried out to the ball diamond. Everyone was there. Even Abe, who had gone home at noon and returned with a worn baseball glove.

"We don't need you today, Professor." Travis said. "Everybody's here. The teams are even. You'll mess things up."

"What's wrong with the Professor playing?" Reg asked.

"Yeah," Brandon Carter joined in. "He plays all right."

"We don't need him today," Travis came back.

Abe looked at me.

I swallowed hard and wet my lips. "I told him he could play."

"Well, he can't. He made his choice last Saturday at the mine. He didn't want to be with us then. He can't be with us now. Besides, the teams have to be even," Travis snapped.

"We've played with the teams uneven," Reg pointed out, "when *you* wanted to."

"He doesn't play," Travis said loudly. "We made a little deal with the Professor on Saturday, didn't we, Professor?" He glanced at Wesley for support. Wesley scratched the back of his head, shrugged and then nodded, siding with Travis. "We told you, Professor, that if you wanted to play with us, you'd have to go into the mine."

The guys on my team looked from Travis and Wesley to me. "Going in the mine doesn't have anything to do with baseball," I came back. "And he went into the mine as far as the rest of us did."

"We don't need him today," Travis announced warmly. "The teams are even without him."

I hesitated, not sure what to do or say, but it was during that moment of hesitation that Abe turned and walked away. "Abe," I called after him. He continued to walk. "Abe, come back." He kept walking. "It wouldn't hurt if he played," I said, turning on Travis.

Travis glared back at me. "We don't need him."

"You're just afraid we'll beat you if he plays with us," Brandon burst out.

Travis stomped over to Brandon and gave him a shove. "Let's see if you can beat us, fat boy. You've got Chris today. He's better than the Professor any day."

"We'll beat you," I threatened. "Without Abe we'll beat you. And then he can play with us after this."

We lost that day. It wasn't even close. I don't think even Abe could have helped us. When the game was over, I hurried into the school building, made my way into the basement, put on the old boxing gloves, and began pounding the battered, misshapen burlap bag until the sweat ran down my face.

"Who you punching today?" Abe asked from the door.

I stopped and faced him. I hadn't seen him standing there until he spoke. I wiped the sweat from my face with the tail of my shirt, panting and trying to catch my breath. "I'm just practicing." I looked down at the floor. "I'm sorry about this afternoon. I wanted you to play."

"I know."

"Some day he's not going to get his way. One of these days I'm going to—" I bit off the threat and smashed my fist into the punching bag.

He shook his head. "It doesn't matter. I don't care about playing ball, not here. It's no big deal."

"Travis doesn't want you to play because you play better than he does. It doesn't have anything to do with your not going in the mine. At first I thought it was because—" I coughed. "Well, because you seemed a little different, not like most kids in Baker's Bend. But that isn't it. You're the only guy that ever struck out Travis Williams. He won't ever give you a chance."

"Who're you punching?"

I shook my head. "I'm just practicing," I said through clenched teeth.

"Practicing so you can fight Travis?"

I thought a moment. "Maybe."

"With some coaching, you might be able to take Travis on. I could teach you something."

I returned to my punching, lashing out viciously at the burlap bag.

"You need to lead more with your left," Abe coached from the door. "And keep your elbows in. Hold your right a little lower than your left. It's got to be ready for that knockout punch."

I did what he said, sensing that he did know what he was talking about. He coached me for over an hour. At first he stood in the doorway and called out instructions. Then he put on the other gloves and gave me a real target to work with. It was surprising how much I was able to improve.

"You're getting the hang of it," Abe commented when we were finished. "Of course, you were a bit of a natural to start with. With some more practice, I figure you could take most anyone in town. And you'd have to believe you could do it."

"What about you? Maybe you could take on anybody in town too. If you believed you could."

He looked away and shook his head. "I'll never be a boxer."

"Because you promised your mom?"

"Maybe."

"Why'd you promise your mom you wouldn't box?" I asked Abe as we were walking home. "Especially if you know about boxing and you seem to like it?"

Abe stopped under a giant sycamore tree, staring down at the ground. "It was on account of my older brother, Isaac," he said after a long pause. "He was good. Some people said he was going to make it as a professional fighter. That's what the coaches said, not just the kids. Nobody could beat him."

Abe paused. He leaned against the trunk of the tree and began picking at the bark with his fingernail. "Then he started running with a gang. Everybody on the streets was afraid of him. Sometimes he'd come home with his knuckles smashed up and bleeding. His coach told him to stop fighting in the street. He told him he should prove how good he was in the ring, not in a back alley. Isaac wouldn't listen. His coach refused to coach him anymore. Isaac got mean. There were a lot of guys on the street that didn't like him.

"One night he got in a fight and beat up a guy pretty good. Later the kid's brother went looking for Isaac. When he found him, he used a knife on him. Isaac was only seventeen," Abe said in a hoarse whisper. For a moment I thought he might cry. "He never became a professional. No one remembers him now. Except me."

"He got killed?"

Abe nodded, still staring down at the ground.

"Your mom was afraid the same thing would happen to you?"

Abe shook his head. "*I* was afraid the same thing would happen to me. I was always afraid someone was going to hit me. And some people thought because I was Isaac's brother that I should be a good fighter too. I didn't want anyone thinking that I was like Isaac. I'm not like Isaac. He wasn't afraid to get beat up a bit, in the ring or on the street. That just made him mean and fight harder. I couldn't do that." He heaved a sigh. "Mom was worried about me. She wondered if I'd turn out like Isaac. She knew she was dying of cancer. I promised her then that I wouldn't be a boxer or a fighter. But I was afraid. That's why

I promised. Sometimes I wish I could fight, though. Then guys like Travis wouldn't push me around. I wouldn't have to walk away."

I looked over at him, and our eyes met. He turned away, and we started toward home.

"I wanted to go into the mine Saturday," he announced suddenly.

"What?"

"I really did want to go in. I still do."

"Then you're crazy."

"Mines give me the creeps." He stopped. "Even more than boxing."

"So why would you want to go into the Baker Mine?"

"To find something out."

"About the ghosts?"

"Not exactly. I don't really believe in ghosts."

"You don't figure Jake Baker got left behind in the mine?"

He hesitated and then shook his head. "But it's more than that. I worry about my dad."

"What does your dad have to do with anything at the Baker Mine?"

"When I was just a little kid," he began reluctantly, "my father and uncle died in a mine accident. It was a cave-in. I don't remember much about it. I just remember that Dad never came home again. I kinda remember the funeral, a lot of people crying and wearing black. But I don't remember seeing Dad's body or the casket. Mom wouldn't talk about it much. Whenever I talked to her about it, she'd start crying." He hesitated.

"I started wondering if they ever dug Dad out of that mine, but—" He shook his head. "I talked to Isaac about it. He said, 'Sure they dug them out, stupid.' But he said it like someone trying to get me to believe in Santa Claus or the Tooth Fairy. And when I asked him if he had seen Dad in the casket, he said he hadn't."

"So you figure your dad's still buried back in Pennsylvania like Jake Baker's buried up in the Baker mine?"

"It's kinda like that. I used to have this dream. It was always the same." Abe stared straight ahead as though he were seeing something, but there was nothing there. "I would be standing in front of a mine, and I could hear Dad and Uncle Jack calling to me, begging me to get them out." He coughed but it sounded more like a sob. "In my dream I never dared go into the mine. I would just stand there staring into the black hole, shaking and sweating. The only time I've felt like that was in my dream." He paused. "Until Saturday. That's how I felt Saturday. It was like my dream came to life and I was standing in that same mine. I wanted to scream. I just had to get out of there.

"Once I was outside again, I thought of my dream. I used to tell myself that it was just a crazy dream, that I didn't have to worry about anything that happened in a dumb dream. I used to tell myself that if I had really been there when Dad got caught in the cave-in, I would have gone in after him. I wouldn't have left him in there.

"And then Saturday, when Travis told me to go back—" He turned away and wiped at his eyes. "I wanted to go to the back of the mine, to prove that I could. But I couldn't. I was afraid. I knew then that I would have been afraid if Dad had been inside that mine. I would have run away, Jared, just like I did Saturday."

"I'm sorry about your dad and your uncle," I mumbled. "But going into the Baker Mine wouldn't prove anything. I mean, even if your dad is buried back in Pennslyvania, going into the Baker Mine isn't going to dig him out."

He shrugged. "Maybe it was a dumb dream. But it came back again Saturday night. And last night. But it was worse. It had been a long time since I had that dream. Now it doesn't seem like a dream anymore. After Saturday it seems real. Last night I was more scared than I've ever been. I woke up screaming, and that woke up Uncle Reuben and Aunt Ruth." He shook his head. "Now I wish I had gone back in the mine." He looked at me. "I don't like being afraid, Jared. But I'm afraid of a lot of things."

"Everybody's afraid of something." I shrugged. "I'm afraid of different things."

Abe nodded. "I know you are. You're afraid of ghosts. You're afraid of Travis and Wesley."

"Maybe," I grumbled, ashamed that Abe had seen my fear. "But going in that dumb old mine won't change any of that."

Abe thought for a long time and then he spoke. "When my brother Isaac was starting to box, he was supposed to fight this black kid named Samson Stephens. Nobody had ever beaten Samson in three years of boxing. Isaac had watched guys go in the ring against him and get beat up. Most of them got knocked out. They'd step into the ring, all scared and shaking, just waiting for Samson to come pound on them.

"Isaac was supposed to fight Samson in a tournament. He was scared spitless." Abe grinned. "Isaac told me that he almost wet his pants just waiting for his match to begin against Samson. And that made him mad. He decided that he wasn't going to just wait for Samson Stephens to come pound on him. He figured as long as he was going to get beat up he was at least going to go after Samson first.

"As soon as the bell rang, Isaac charged across the ring. Samson was so surprised he hardly got out of his corner. He hadn't expected anybody to go after him." Abe laughed. "Isaac beat him. Knocked him out in the first round. He told me later that once he had knocked Samson out, he wasn't afraid of anybody. Nothing could scare him after that because he had come face to face with the toughest kid he knew."

"Your brother must have been some fighter."

Abe nodded. "I wish I was like him. I don't mean being a fighter. I don't care about that. But I wish I wasn't afraid. Maybe that's why I hate that dream I have, because when I have it I know I'm afraid."

"But the Baker Mine isn't the mine in your dream. And going into the Baker Mine won't make the dream go away."

"But maybe if I could go to the back of the Baker Mine—" He paused and looked over at me, his eyes dark with worry. "Maybe the Baker Mine could be like Isaac facing Samson Stephens. I hope they didn't leave Dad and Uncle Jack in that mine in Pennsylvania. But if they had and I had been there, I would have been too scared to go in after them. I don't want to be scared like that. Maybe it's just something I want to prove to myself."

"So you're going to go back to the Baker Mine?"

Abe thought a long time. "I wish I could."

"Just forget about it, Abe. You're talking crazy."

We were quiet as we started toward home again. When we reached the corner where I usually turned to avoid passing Leon Lucero's place, Abe stopped me. "Do you want to stop and see Leo?" he asked casually.

"Why would I want to stop and see Leo?"

"To talk to him."

"I don't want to talk to him."

"He's not crazy."

"He killed a man."

Abe shrugged. "That was a long time ago. You don't have to be afraid of him. He's an interesting guy. You'd like talking to him."

"He couldn't tell me anything I'd want to know."

Abe paused. "He's my friend. He wouldn't hurt you."

"Why would you have a friend like Loco Leo?" I demanded.

"He's about the only real friend that I have here in Baker's Bend."

I don't know why I agreed to go with Abe to Leo's place. I was anxious and a bit shaky as we picked our way over the broken walk to Leo's front steps. My mouth was dry and my throat tight as we creaked up the steps and across the squeaking floor to the front door.

Abe hammered on the door with his fist, paused a moment, and then knocked again. "That's so he'll know that it's really someone at the door," he explained. "Instead of just someone trying to bother him."

A moment later I heard someone shuffle to the front door. I could hardly breathe. I wanted to turn and run, but I knew I couldn't, not with Abe there.

The door suddenly flew open, and there stood Leo. He glanced first at Abe and then his gaze settled over me like a confining web. It was the first time I had ever had a good close look at him. He had a thin, dark face, creased with wrinkles, and a long scar that went from his right ear to the corner of his mouth. The scar had twisted and distorted his face into a permanent frown.

His eyes were dark, almost black, and one opened wider than the other. It was that wide eye that seemed to stare out and pierce right through me.

"What do you want?" Leo demanded, looking squarely at me.

I couldn't open my mouth to speak, and I was sure I was going to faint right there on Leo's front porch.

"I came to talk to you." Abe spoke up like he was talking to his aunt or uncle. "Jared wanted to come along," he added, nodding toward me.

Leo continued to stare at me with his wide eye, and then he rubbed the back of his rough, callused hand along the gray whiskers growing on his jaw. He adjusted the faded pants he was wearing, and then he nodded his head for us to enter.

Abe stepped in first, and I followed him, looking around. I expected to see dirt, junk, and broken furniture everywhere. I was surprised to see that the inside of the house was simple, plain but clean. There wasn't a lot of furniture in the front room and it was all old and worn, but everything was neat. The floor was just bare boards, but it was swept and scrubbed.

Leo led us from the front room down a long hall past several closed doors into a rather large kitchen. Other than a wall full of cupboards, all that was in the kitchen was a small gas stove, a sink, a tiny table with four chairs set about it, and an old refrigerator.

"Pull up a chair," Leo ordered, returning to his plate on the tiny kitchen table. He picked up his fork and began eating fried eggs and bacon. I thought it strange that he would have breakfast food for supper.

Abe and I sat down. Leo took a few bites, and then with his mouth full, he glowered across the table at me and asked, "You didn't bring any dead cats this time?"

I gulped and shook my head.

He swallowed and ran his tongue around inside his mouth. "You're Peter Slocombe's boy, aren't you?"

I nodded once.

"I knew your grandpa. He was a few years older than me. He was a decent kind of fellow. I don't figure he would have wanted any grandkid of his hanging dead cats on people's porches. What do *you* think?"

I nodded and twisted uncomfortably in my chair.

"I'm sorry about the cat," I rasped hoarsely. I swallowed hard and wet my lips. "The other guys made me do it."

"They *made* you do it? Do you let other people decide what *you're* going to do?"

I twisted in my chair and shrugged.

"Do you know how to talk?"

I nodded.

"Did you come here just to watch me eat, or did you have something else on your mind?"

"Actually," Abe began, "we came here to—"

"I'm talking to Mr. Slocombe," Leo cut him off. "I want to know why *he's* here."

"Abe said you knew something about the Baker Mine," I burst out, unable to take my eyes from Leo.

Leo stared at me. "Maybe I know something. Depends on what you want to know."

"About the ghosts in the mine. If there are any."

Leo returned to his eating. "You shouldn't even be hanging around those old mines," he said after a while, still eating his strange supper. "They're dangerous. Any one of them could cave in on top of you. If you got caught back in there, nobody would get you out. Fifty years ago they might have dug you out, but not today. There's no equipment around here that could dig you out in time. And even if there was, it would take forever to get the equipment up the mountain."

"You worked there, didn't you?"

Leo shook his head. "Not in the mines. I just hauled supplies up the mountain. With pack mules."

"Are there men buried in the mine?"

Leo glared at me again with his wide eye. "There were some that *were* buried there. Not any more."

"Jake Baker?"

Leo wiped his plate clean with a piece of bread and pushed back from the table. "I've got things to do," he announced gruffly, ending our conversation abruptly. "I don't have time to waste talking about fool mines and dead men's bones." He stared down at me with his wide, searching eye. "Leave the Baker Mine be, boy."

"So you think it's haunted."

"Nothing good ever came from it. I know."

It was dark when Abe and I left Leo's place. We didn't speak to each other until we were far away from his house, where he couldn't hear us.

I swallowed hard and dug my fists deep into my pockets. "I'm afraid of the mine. I don't care who knows that."

"But you're afraid of a lot of things. Maybe you'll always be afraid."

"What's that supposed to mean?"

"Just something I see in you. I see it in myself. Maybe if we went to the mine—"

"I won't go to the mine with you," I cut him off.

"You heard what Leo said. We ought to stay away from there."

He looked at me sadly and then turned and started for home.

Chapter 11

Ever since we went to Leo's together, Abe stopped by a lot. After school he helped me do my janitor work and coached me while I boxed. He helped me with my chores at home. But he didn't ever ask to play ball again. Once I asked him about it. "We could use your pitching, Abe," I said as we were walking home from school one late afternoon. "Chris and Reg and some of the other guys have asked about you too."

Abe shook his head. "I don't care about baseball anymore. Besides, the teams are even without me."

"I think I could get the guys to let you play."

He shook his head. "Travis doesn't want me. And he always gets his way."

"Who says he can always have his way?"

Abe smiled at me. "You're not afraid of him anymore?"

"I didn't ever say I was afraid of him," I bristled, flinching a little.

"You'd dare fight him? Because that's what he'd make you do if he didn't get his way. You'd probably have to fight Wesley too."

I wanted to tell Abe that I wasn't afraid of either one of them, but I knew it would be a lie. And Abe would know it was a lie. I kicked at a pebble and muttered, "Well, if you want to play, I can talk to the others."

He shook his head. "I don't think much about baseball any more."

Several times I went with Abe to Leo's house. He was always friendly with Abe, but he seemed suspicious of me, studying me with his wide, staring eye and grumbling at me for no reason. I felt safe while Abe was around, though, and I liked hearing Leo talk about Baker's Bend and how it had been years ago.

Late one Friday afternoon Leo was getting ready to haul a load of scrap metal to Fairview. He invited Abe and me to go with him.

I thought of the three of us driving down the streets of Baker's Bend in Leo's old truck. I knew everybody would stare at us, whisper, and laugh. "I've got some chores to do at home," I mumbled as Abe climbed into the truck. "I better not go."

Leo stared at me and then a taunting smile twisted his face. "You don't want to be seen riding around with the crazy man, is that it?"

I fidgeted uneasily. "No, I've got chores."

He nodded. "Just don't leave me any dead cats while we're gone, Mr. Slocombe."

I shook my head, backing away. Leo started the

engine, and he and Abe pulled away. Just then Chris Winder and Reg Ferguson rode by on their bikes. They slammed on their brakes and skidded to a stop.

"What were you doing in there?" Chris gasped. I glanced back over my shoulder at the Mansion. "Oh, I go over there sometimes."

"What for?" Reg demanded.

I shrugged. "I've talked to Leo a few times. He's not like I used to think."

"You talk to Loco Leo?" Chris asked, squinting at me.

"I went over with Abe once. Leo's not–" I stopped and thought. "He doesn't scare me much now that I know him some."

"You keep hanging around with Loco Leo and you'll be crazy too, Slocombe," Chris warned. "My mom told me to stay clear of him."

"Do you hang around much with the Professor?" Reg questioned.

I thought a moment and then nodded. "A little."

"Is he your friend?"

"He's all right."

"You pick some weird friends," Chris said, shaking his head.

The next Saturday morning I was up early doing my chores, scattering straw about the freshly mucked-out barn floor and feeding the cows and calves. That's where Megan found me.

"What we going to do today?" she asked as she wandered into the barn and perched on a one-legged stool. "You said we could do something fun today," she reminded me of a promise I had made to her a few days back.

"What did you have in mind?" I asked, walking past her and pulling one of her ponytails.

"Anything. As long as it's real fun."

"Do you want to play catch?"

"Something funner than that."

"Well, give me an idea."

She jumped up and followed me outside. "Let's go swimming."

"How many times do I have to tell you, you don't know how to swim."

"You could teach me."

I shook my head. "The pond's not for little girls, Meg."

"I'm not afraid," she insisted as I began throwing hay down from the stack to the calves in the corral.

"It doesn't have anything to do with being afraid," I replied. "Some things just aren't smart."

"Are you afraid of the pond?"

"Not for me."

Megan looked up at me. "You're not afraid of anything. I wish I was like that." She smiled. "But it's nice having a brother who's not afraid of things. You aren't afraid, are you, Jared?"

"Don't worry about me," I sputtered.

"You're *not* afraid, are you?" she asked, wrinkling her stubby nose. I could tell that she really wanted to know.

"Afraid of what?" I grumbled.

She shrugged. "Of anything."

"I'm not afraid, Meg. Don't worry about it . And don't ask any more dumb questions." But deep inside I felt sick for lying.

Later in the morning, after I'd played a while with Meg and she'd gone off with one of her friends, Abe dropped by. He was serious as he came up the gravel driveway. "I'm going to the mine today," he said quietly as he leaned against the corral fence.

I stared at him. "What are you talking about?"

"I keep having the dream about my dad and uncle."

"It's just a dream, Abe."

"You think there are ghosts in the mine."

"But Leo said nobody was in the mine anymore. He should know."

"Do you believe that?"

I stared at him without answering.

"Will you come with me?" he asked.

I hesitated.

"I'll go alone."

I swallowed. "Abe, your uncle and dad didn't get left in that mine back in Pennsylvania. I'm sure of it."

"Maybe. I've got to prove that to myself. Maybe the dream will go away."

"But, Abe–"

"And most of all I want to prove that I'm not afraid. Isaac would go in the mine."

"You said you didn't want to be like Isaac."

"I don't want to be a fighter like him. But I don't want to be afraid. He wasn't afraid."

"Well, I'm afraid." As soon as I said those words, I remembered what I'd told Megan that same morning. I winced and looked away. I thought a moment. "I'll walk up with you, but I won't go into the mine. I don't have anything to prove."

Abe looked at me. He knew I was lying, but he didn't say anything.

Jumping down from the fence, I went into the house for a flashlight. It was a bit after noon when we reached Baker Pond and headed up the winding mine path, hardly pausing to catch our breath. Panting and sweating, we continued up the mountain, reaching the mine by one-thirty. Clenching the red plastic flashlight that I had borrowed from Mom's kitchen drawer, I stared into the gaping mouth of the Baker Mine.

Abe looked over at me. It was an invitation to go with him, all the invitation that he would give.

"Are you sure about this, Abe?"

His face was pale. He nodded once. I felt sorry

for him, and I guess I knew I liked him, although I hadn't ever admitted that to anyone. I knew it wasn't right to let him go alone. I thought of Megan. "Let's go," I whispered.

"You don't have anything to prove," he said.

"Maybe I do." I blinked nervously. "Let's get it over with," I said, staring into the mine with my heart pounding painfully in my chest. Switching on the flashlight, I forced myself to go into the mine, and the blackness closed about Abe and me.

I don't know where I found my courage. Perhaps it was just stupidity. But I entered the mine with Abe, keeping my eyes riveted to the comfort of the bobbing glow from the flashlight and trying not to notice the cold damp walls, the bowed and rotting timbers, and the piles of rock and dirt that had fallen from the ceiling over the years.

Before we had gone a hundred yards, Abe stopped. I could hear his teeth chatter. "I don't know if I can, Jared. Maybe we'd better go back."

I wanted to agree, but I didn't. "We've come this far, Abe. We can make it. Then we can forget this crazy place."

For a long time Abe didn't answer. Then finally he shuffled forward, feeling his way along the wall of the tunnel while I held the light.

"The tunnel forks about halfway back," I whispered.

"That's where the miners are supposed to be buried?"

"I think so."

We whispered back and forth, asking questions and guessing answers. We tried everything to keep our minds busy. When we came to the fork in the mine, I peered down the black tunnel to my right. Twenty feet from where I stood the right tunnel was blocked off by a huge mound of dirt, rock, and cracked, twisted timbers. "That's the cave-in," I quavered. I strained to listen, but I heard nothing beyond that wall of earth. "Nobody's dug those miners out. Those miners are still back there."

"Let's follow the left tunnel, Jared."

"I think this place is haunted, Abe."

He didn't answer. He just moved forward, pushing deeper into the Baker Mine.

I was shivering when we reached the end of the left tunnel. We stopped and turned around, peering back into the blackness from where we had just come. The light from outside the mine entrance had disappeared long ago because the tunnel curved just before the fork in the mine. Outside the circle of my tiny yellow light we were completely encased in blackness.

Abe dropped to his knees and began gathering rocks. He stacked four of them, one on top of another.

"Now they'll know we were here," he announced, his voice shaking slightly.

"Who will know?"

"Anybody who comes back here."

"Nobody's going to come back here. Nobody cares that we came back here."

"I care. We made it."

When Abe's pile was finished, we started back, moving quickly. I wanted to be free of this place. We stumbled along, forcing ourselves not to break into a run.

When we returned to the fork in the mine, we paused and stared into the right tunnel. "Let's go, Abe. Let's get out of here," I coaxed.

"They were down there, weren't they?" he asked.

"If anybody was ever buried, they're buried behind that rock and dirt."

Without answering, Abe took my flashlight and crept toward the mound of rock and dirt blocking off the right tunnel. "Hey, there's an opening up at the top," he called back.

"What?" I croaked.

He turned to face me. "There's an opening. I think we can crawl through."

"Crawl through? For what? Do you know what's back there?"

Before I could say another word, Abe was scrambling up the mound of dirt and squeezing through an opening at the top. He, along with the light, disappeared.

"Abe!" I called out. "Abe, it's stupid to go in there!" I thought for sure Abe had gone crazy. Just a little while before, he was the one who had wanted to turn back. Now he wouldn't leave. Maybe it was the ghosts keeping him there.

I turned around and was about to race out of the mine, leaving Abe behind, when the light reappeared in the opening and Abe called down to me. "You can make it, easy. Come on, Jared."

"Are there—" I gulped and caught my breath. "Do you see any bodies, any skeletons?"

"Come and see."

I didn't know anyone who had gone into that tunnel. I didn't want to go, but I didn't want to stand there alone in the dark, either. Against my will I crawled up the pile of dirt and rock. It wasn't until my head was brushing against the rocky ceiling that I could clearly see the narrow passage. From the floor of the mine it had been almost hidden.

"Abe, this is crazy."

"It's not as bad as it looks. Really. We've come this far. We can't turn back now."

Taking a deep breath, I squeezed into the opening and clawed my way over the pile of dirt and rock, finally tumbling down the the other side just behind Abe. For a moment I lay still, listening. Then slowly

I pushed myself to my feet. Taking the flashlight from Abe, I directed its pale yellow light back toward the small opening and then down the tunnel. I expected to see a dozen skeletons sprawled all over the tunnel floor. There was nothing.

"This is where they would have been," Abe whispered. "They were buried in this section of the tunnel. If they had left them, they would be right here." He sounded excited, relieved.

"Okay, we looked," I said. "Now let's get out of here before this whole place falls in on us." I looked about me, shining the light. More timbers had been used to hold up the walls and ceilings in this tunnel. And the structure seemed weaker. There were many more places where dirt and rock had caved in.

"We've got to go to the end," Abe said.

"Abe!" I protested. "We're crazy to be here now."

"Wait here and I'll go."

"Abe!" I clutched his arm and pulled him back.

He looked at me. "I've got to know, Jared. We've come this far. I've got to know. I didn't turn back at the front of the cave when I wanted to. You kept me going. I can't turn back now. I'm not so scared any more. But I don't want to be afraid of anything in this mine. I've got to go all the way to the back."

"But, Abe," I protested, "this whole creaky, crazy old mine could fall down on us. And no one knows we're here."

"Listen!" he said, holding up his hand.

I stopped breathing, straining to hear. There was something whistling or moaning from the tunnel. "What is it?" I gasped.

"It sounds like wind."

"In the back of a mine?"

We both continued to strain our ears.

"Could it be them?" I rasped. "The miners' ghosts?"

Abe started down the tunnel. I don't know why, but I followed him. After a few hundred feet, we stopped. The strange sound continued to come from the depths of the mine. I could feel my courage wither inside me.

Abe started forward with me right behind him, the noise growing louder and louder. It was like rushing water. Suddenly the tunnel widened. A stream of water dropped from a hole above and cascaded down the left side of the tunnel to disappear into a gaping hole below. It was a regular underground stream, perhaps the beginning of Baker Creek.

Reaching out, I touched the icy water. Slowly some of my fear left me.

"There's air coming from there," Abe spoke, holding his hand up toward the opening.

The tunnel was rough and slanted toward the opening where the water entered. Abe climbed up with the flashlight. "There's a cave," he called back.

"The water is coming from another cave. The wind is coming from there. This must open to the outside."

"Let's go, Abe."

We crept past the water and pushed onward into the blackness of the mine. It seemed forever, but finally we reached the end of the tunnel. Abe shined the light across the jagged rock. There was no mistaking it. This was where the last miners had dug. There were no other cave-ins, no other secret graves. The tunnel had never gone deeper than this. We had explored the entire mine. No one had been left in the mine. There were no ghosts.

I dropped to my knees and gathered a pile of rocks. As I stood, I announced, "Abe, we're probably the only people alive who have ever been back here since the mine closed. We've done something no one else has done."

"Now we can leave."

When we could finally see the mine's entrance, we began to jog toward the light. We didn't slow down until we burst from the mine's damp, clinging blackness and flung ourselves into the warm light of the sun.

"We made it!" Abe called out.

I dropped to the ground and gasped for breath, feeling my whole body tremble.

"We made it!" Abe repeated.

I swallowed and looked up at him. He turned and started down the mountain, and I followed him.

Chapter 12

I think you've got the hang of it," Abe grinned at me as we put the boxing gloves away the next Monday afternoon. "You're starting to remind me of Isaac. Before he turned mean," he added quickly.

"It's one thing to practice down here," I muttered, looking about the old coal bin with the home-made punching bag dangling from the ceiling. "It's a whole different game facing – " I stopped and heaved a sigh.

"You mean Travis?"

I thought a moment and shook my head. "All I've proved before was that my nose will bleed pretty good."

"It's different now, Jared. You're better."

"Chris said he saw you out pitching the other day," I remarked, changing the subject.

His cheeks reddened. "I like to think about playing back in Philly."

We started up the stairs to begin cleaning. "Oh, Leo asked me to have you drop by sometime. Do you want to tonight?"

I glanced over at Abe. "What does he want with me?" I asked nervously.

"He says he has something to show you."

I wasn't anxious to visit Leo that evening, but Abe coaxed while we worked and then later as we walked home. "I can only stop for a minute," I explained, finally giving in.

I wasn't exactly scared as Abe and I stood on the Mansion's front porch and banged on Leo's door, but there was a nervous rumbling in my stomach that made me fidget and fret. I heard Leo's shuffling steps and then the front door opened. Leo nodded at both of us and grunted, "I wondered if you'd stop by this evening."

He led us through the huge front room and down the long hall to the kitchen. He motioned for us both to sit at the table, and then he went over to an old leather chest that sat in the corner next to the cupboards. It hadn't been there on my first visit. Leo gripped one of the leather handles and dragged the chest over to the table.

"You've heard all the stories that scared boys tell each other about the mine," he commented, glancing at me. "I thought you might like to see something real." Slowly he unsnapped the lid and pushed it back.

I gaped inside. One by one Leo pulled out the chest's contents. There was an old battered miner's cap, with a light in front. There was a miner's pick, a pair of leather boots, a blackened kerosene lantern, and some old blasting caps. There was a small leather bag filled with ore.

I reached for the bag of ore and dug my fingers into the gold dirt. "Do you suppose this is worth much?" I inquired.

"It's not a rich ore," Leo answered, shaking his head. "It would take more work to get the gold out of that little dab than it's worth. But that's ore from the mine. Probably dug out by Horace Baker himself."

Leo pulled out some old work clothes with H. Baker written in the collar of the shirt. There was a long knife in a leather sheath and a small black revolver with the hammer broken off.

"Where'd you get all this stuff?" I asked, my eyes wide with curiosity as I hefted the revolver.

Leo raised his gaze toward the ceiling. "In the attic. Years ago."

He reached down into the trunk again and pulled out a leather valise. Two leather belt straps kept the valise closed. Leo unbuckled them and pulled out some crinkled yellowed papers. "As near as I can tell, these are some of the records Horace kept, written in his own hand." He reached in again. "But this is what I thought you'd be interested in." He pulled out three black-and-white photographs, each about six inches by ten inches. One was a picture of a dozen or so miners, holding their picks and wearing their miner hats while they sat on the steps of a wooden two-story building.

"This was taken up there, in front of Horace's place up the canyon."

"Is that the big building that's still up there?" I questioned.

"The very one. Do you see the boy in the front? That's me."

"Why, you weren't much older than Abe and me."

Leo nodded and pushed the second picture toward me. It was a picture of a huge, beautiful home with a young woman in a white dress standing on the front steps. "That's this very house. It was in better shape then."

I studied the lady's face. She was pretty and not very old. Probably in her twenties. "Who is she?" I asked.

"That's Mrs. Baker, Horace's wife. She was a pretty thing, young and innocent. A nice one too. I always liked Mrs. Baker. And I always kinda felt sorry for her and never knew why."

Leo handed me the next picture. Two unsmiling, bearded men stood in front of the mouth of a mine. One of them had his hand on the back of the neck of a huge dog. "That's Jake and Horace," Leo explained simply. "And that's Jake's wolf dog."

I glanced back at the picture of the Mansion and Mrs. Baker. "But they're both old men," I observed.

"Lots older than she is," I added, pointing to Mrs. Baker.

"Horace was at least twenty years older than his wife. I don't know why she married him. Maybe it was the money." He shrugged. "There were a lot of people who wondered about that."

"It's all real, isn't it?" I asked.

Leo nodded. "I remember those days. They were good days. Happy days. I loved packing supplies up to the mine. I loved sitting around jawin' with the miners. They were a good lot." He shook his head. "Then everything went sour." He turned a cool glare on me. "The mine's no good now. Nobody should bother it."

"Abe and I went into the mine last Saturday, all the way to the back," I said, glancing over at Abe, who nodded.

Leo studied us both. "That's what Abe told me. To my knowledge, no one's gone to the back of those mines since they closed down." He shook his head. "No one."

"We left markers," I said. "You could go back and see for yourself."

"Maybe you were fool enough to go in and place a marker. But I'm not fool enough to follow you in. Only a fool would go in there." He was gruff and irritable. Suddenly he laughed. The laugh started out as a chuckle, but the crazy chuckle grew louder until it filled the huge kitchen. Then the laughter stopped as suddenly as it had started. “Did you find your ghosts?”

I shook my head.

“There are no ghosts in the Baker Mine,” Leo muttered disgustedly. “There never have been.” A smile cracked Leo’s scar-twisted frown. “But the stories are right about one thing. Jake didn’t ever leave that mountain. He’s still there. Someplace. Or what’s left of him is still there.”

“Some folks say Jake Baker’s buried in the mine,” I said. “Folks say he went in the mine with his wolf dog the morning it gave way. And now his ghost and his dog wander around the mines and mountain, haunting everything.”

“You believe that?”

I thought a moment. “We didn’t see anyplace where he might have been buried,” I said uneasily. “We’ve been in the mine. Do you think he’s buried there?”

A crooked smile twisted Leo’s dark face. “It took more than two weeks to dig back to where the miners were.”

“But the mine is still caved in.”

“That happened later, years after the mine closed down for good. That isn’t the original cave-in.”

“Then they did get them out?” Abe asked.

Leo studied him a moment. He nodded once.

"Yes, they dug them out. But they were all dead. All but two of them had lived through the cave-in. They probably lived close to a week, shut up in a section of the tunnel. But they all suffocated because nobody could get to them in time. I helped pack the bodies down the mountain, nine of them. But Jake Baker wasn't one of them."

"So Jake Baker *is* still in the mine," I burst out.

"Everybody that was there got dug out."

"But Skip Manning's grandpa claims he saw Jake's wolf dog five years after the mine closed down. He said there was no mistaking that dog."

"And was Jake with it?"

I swallowed and shrugged my shoulders. "But people say they were always together. Skip's grandpa claims he saw a ghost when he saw that wolf dog."

"I've seen the dog myself. It was as wild as any wolf. And it moved like a ghost. But it was alive. It didn't die in that mine. Neither did Jake."

"What do you mean?"

"Horace Baker was as crooked as a dog's hind leg. He wasn't bringing enough out of those mines to make them pay. He was making his money on the rich men from the east who were buying stock in the mine. They were the fools that kept the mine going as long as it did. Horace kept promising them that the profits would soon be pouring in. Some of them made a little money. But it was stolen money, stolen from other suckers just like themselves who were greedy and willing to trust a crook like Horace Baker.

"Jake must have known Horace was running a crooked business. Jake didn't care about the money. He only cared about the mine. Horace must have been afraid that his brother was going to give him away. When the mine caved in, everyone knew Jake was in there. And it was no accident that Jake was in there. Right where Horace wanted him. But Jake walked away."

"How?" Abe questioned, speaking for the first time.

He studied Abe a moment. "Your pa was a miner. What is a miner supposed to do when everything starts crashing down?"

"If he's in a safe place, he just stays put and hopes his air and water hold out. Sooner or later someone will dig him out."

Leo shook his head. "But Jake didn't stay with the others. He went deeper into the mine. The others might have lived, too, if they had followed him."

"How do you know? And if he did escape, where is Jake now?"

"That same morning I was leading a string of mules with supplies up the mountain. I had stopped off the trail to rest when I saw Horace and Jake off in the trees. Jake had his dog then. They were arguing. I didn't pay them much mind because they were always arguing. Then I heard Jake accuse Horace of trying to kill him. They said horrible things to each other. I got scared and started up the mountain with my pack mules, leaving those two behind, shouting and cursing at each other. I didn't know anything about the cave-in then. Later, when I reached the mine, everybody was rushing about because of the cave-in. I forgot all about Horace and Jake's argument.

"As they were digging for those miners, they began to suspect that the cave-in was no accident. There had been an explosion. Jake was never found in the mine. He had just vanished. That's why people started talking about his ghost. It wasn't until later that I started putting things together and realized that I had seen Jake and Horace arguing *after* the mine had caved in."

"If Jake did go into the mine that morning, but you saw him later that same morning, then there must be another way out," Abe said.

"Some years ago I was poking around up there and discovered something that Jake must have always known. There are several mines up there. Half a dozen. But the first one, the very first one that Horace and Jake started, is above the main mine. It's opening is farther north, and it's the only one of the mines that enters the mountain from the east. It goes in at an angle, and drops down steeply."

"Is that the small one, the one that's partly covered over with brush?" I asked, leaning forward in my chair.

Leo nodded. "Brush has covered the entrance for years now."

"I've seen it before. I've never gone in more than a few feet, but I know where it is."

"Well, part of that first mine passes through a natural cave cut through the mountain by an underground creek. Part of that water passage is big enough for a man to climb through, and it cuts right through both mines. If you went to the back of the mine, you had to pass that creek."

"We passed it," Abe said.

"I followed that old mine to the very back, where the creek runs. I entered that water passage and followed it down twenty or thirty feet and found myself standing in the main mine. That's when I figured that that was how Jake got out of there. He knew about that passageway into the old mine.

"The night Horace left Baker's Bend, his wife hanged herself in this house. I figure she found out what Jake had known for a long time—that Horace was a crook, that he would do anything for money. Even kill. Maybe she suspected what had happened to Jake.

"Horace headed for Peru. Some say he started

another mine." Leo attempted a smile but it looked more like a snarl.

"What happened to him?"

Leo shrugged. "Some say there was a mine disaster down there and he was buried alive. Others say he went crazy and was put away. Some say he got drunk and was killed in a fight. Others say he hanged himself, just like his wife did."

"What do you say?" I ventured.

Leo stared at me. "I don't know what happened to Horace Baker after he left Baker's Bend."

"But you think you know what happened to his brother Jake?"

"I have my suspicions." Leo stood up and walked over to the corner where his gnarled walking stick leaned against the wall. He grabbed it and brought it over to me. "Take it," he directed.

Reluctantly I took the walking stick.

"There were two things Jake Baker was never without. His wolf dog and his walking stick. The morning I saw Horace and Jake arguing, Jake had both his dog *and* his walking stick. Do you see what's carved in that stick?" he asked.

I looked down at the stick and saw two letters carved in the wood—JB. I looked up at Leo.

"I found this, years after the mine closed, stuck down in a crack between two huge boulders. I saw that very stick many times in Jake's own hands. It didn't just fall between those boulders. It had been hidden."

"Are you saying Horace killed his brother and hid him somewhere on the mountain?"

He glared at me and nodded. "The wolf dog didn't ever leave the mountain because his master didn't ever leave the mountain. And I suspect if there had been another man that that dog trusted, he would have led the man to Jake's grave."

"Did you ever tell the police?"

"It wasn't until years later that I figured out what I'm telling you now." He began putting things back into the chest. "Besides, I don't tell the police nothing." He sucked in a huge breath of air. "If Jake Baker haunts anything, it's not that miserable mine up there. He would have gone looking for the cowardly cheat he had for a brother." A smile twisted his face. "Maybe he found him." He turned his gaze on me. "But if you went in that mine Saturday, you were a fool."

"I'm still glad we went into the mine," I said quietly to Abe as we left the Mansion and started home.

"Are you still afraid of ghosts?" he asked.

I thought a moment. "There's something creepy about the canyon. And the mine is dangerous."

"But do you still believe in the ghosts?"

I shook my head. "Not now. Not like I used to."

"They didn't leave my dad and uncle in the mine

back in Pennsylvania. I'm sure they dug them out. I'm glad we went in the Baker Mine because I don't feel as scared any more."

"I wouldn't want to go back," I admitted.

"Neither would I," Abe said, shaking his head. "But if I knew my dad was in that mine, or another one, I wouldn't be afraid to go in after him. I haven't had the dream again. Maybe I'll never have the dream again."

Chapter 13

May crept by. In the afternoon of the Saturday before the end of school, Abe and I were walking down Miner Street past the Mansion when we saw Travis, Wesley, and Skip coming up the street toward us, lugging an old rusty bucket. I nodded in their direction but was anxious to keep walking.

"Hey, Professor," Travis called out, "do you want to help us leave a present for Loco Leo?"

Wesley and Skip giggled. Abe and I moved closer and looked into the bucket. It was half full of fresh horse manure.

"He'll catch you for sure if you try to leave that on his front porch," I warned. "He's always around on Saturdays."

Travis laughed and shook his head. "Not today. We saw him heading toward Fairview in his truck not twenty minutes ago."

"We're going to leave this on his front porch," Wesley said.

"Why?" I demanded.

"He's getting really ornery these days," Skip spoke up with a grin. "I walked past his place yesterday with my little brother, and he chased me halfway down the street."

"We don't like him bothering us," Travis said.

"What did you do first?" I asked .

"I threw one little rock at his house, at the second story. It didn't hurt him any. He doesn't use anything in that old barn above the first floor. I don't even think he owns that place. He just lives there because nobody cares." He grinned. "We didn't see Leo coming down the street behind us. He almost caught us and beat us with his stick."

"We're going to teach the old buzzard a lesson," Travis growled.

"Leave him alone!" Abe blurted out.

Every eye turned toward him.

"He doesn't bother people if they leave him alone." He spoke fiercely.

"Professor," Travis came back, "don't you tell us what to do." He smiled. "I don't care if Loco Leo is your uncle."

The others laughed.

"Leave him alone," Abe ordered, stepping between him and the Mansion. Travis stared at Abe and pushed past him, giving him a quick shove as he did. Abe reached out, grabbed Travis's arm, and pulled him around. Travis glowered at Abe and then jerked his arm free and lunged for Abe. Abe stepped to the side, and Travis's unchecked momentum caused him to slip and fall.

Wesley jumped forward, grabbed Abe from behind and held him. "You picked the fight, Professor," he growled. "Now don't run from it. Come on, Travis." Wesley released Abe as Travis got to his feet.

Travis grinned and doubled up his fists. "Come on, Professor. Let's see if you can do something besides read your books."

Abe stood for a moment with his hands at his sides. Slowly he shook his head and mumbled, "I don't want any fight."

"You should have thought of that before you started pushing," Travis answered, moving in.

Travis threw a punch that smashed into Abe's shoulder, spinning him partway around. Abe didn't fight back. "Come on, Professor," Travis taunted.

"I don't want to fight," Abe said, backing up.

Wesley stepped forward and pushed Abe toward Travis. Travis lashed out with the flat of his hand, slapping Abe in the face.

Grabbing the side of his face, Abe shouted, "I just want you to leave Leo alone!"

Travis grinned through clenched teeth.

I winced as Travis slapped him again and then kicked him in the seat of the pants, but still Abe wouldn't fight.

"Leave him alone!" I heard myself burst out. "He doesn't want to fight." I stepped between Travis and Abe.

"He wanted to fight a minute ago," Travis argued.

An uncertainty rumbled inside me. "He just doesn't want you messing with Leo." I explained.

"Get out of my way, Slocombe, or you'll get it too."

I didn't move. Suddenly someone grabbed me from behind and pushed me. Whipping around, I faced Wesley. "Back off," Wesley growled. "This is between Travis and the Professor. The Professor's the one that started pushing."

For a moment I imagined myself in the school basement standing by the old burlap punching bag. Many times I had imagined Travis's face on the old burlap bag. But never Wesley's. Wesley was at least twenty pounds heavier and three inches taller than I was. And although Travis and Wesley had never fought, I was sure that Travis wouldn't be able to take Wesley. I had never even considered confronting him.

Slowly I took a step backward away from Wesley. I turned to Travis and Abe. "Come on, Abe," I whispered, "don't let him push you. You know what to do. Don't be afraid."

"What do you mean the Professor knows what to do?" Travis laughed with his fists still up.

"He's a boxer," I blurted out. "He's good too."

"I'm scared," Travis mocked, pretending to shake. "Come on, Professor, show me what you can do."

Abe looked from Travis to me, his eyes wide and frightened. "Come on, you can do it. Get your fists up like you've told me. Move around. Don't be afraid of him."

Suddenly Travis charged. Abe's fists snapped into position and he leaped aside, still glancing from Travis to me as if asking me what he ought to do next.

"Get ready, Abe. You can do it," I coached. More than anything I wanted Abe to fight Travis. And I wanted Abe to win. I wanted to watch Abe plow Travis into the ground. I watched tensely with my fists clenched at my sides and my muscles tight and straining.

Travis charged wildly, angry that Abe had slipped away from him for the second time. Abe's face was white and taut. He looked as though he were in a daze, but he started to dance on his toes with his fists in front of him. He stayed just beyond Travis's reach.

"Hold still, Professor," Wesley ordered. "You're fighting, not playing tag. Get him, Travis."

"Come on, Abe," I pleaded. "Don't let your guard down. Wait for the right punch."

Travis was frustrated, and he lunged forward. Abe lashed out with a left jab to Travis's jaw and followed it up quickly with a right cross to the side of Travis's head. The punches weren't hard ones, but they made

Travis furious. I was sure he had never expected Abe to be able to hit him. His eyes narrowed, his jaw clamped tight, and he rushed at Abe.

Abe froze. Travis smashed into him, knocking him backwards. He stumbled, and Travis charged again. This time Abe went down on the seat of his pants. Travis slapped at him, kicked his legs, and yelled, "Get up, Professor! I want to see you box."

"Come on, Abe," I coaxed. "You got him once. You can do it again. Don't let him push you around."

Travis backed up so that Abe could push himself to his feet, but I could tell by Abe's expression that he wasn't going to fight any more. Travis was on him before he had straightened up. He punched him once in the face. Abe ducked and covered his head and face with his arms. Travis punched and slapped at him angrily.

I knew the fight was over when Travis pushed Abe to the ground again and Abe didn't even attempt to get to his feet. "You're a real mean boxer, Professor," Travis tormented. "You're a real mean machine." He walked over and slapped at his head while he was still down.

"All right, you beat him," I shouted. "Now leave him alone."

"Don't you start up, Slocombe," Travis yelled, pointing a finger at me. "I ought to slap you around. You're the one that told him to fight."

"I just want you to leave Abe alone," I came back.

"Take off, Slocombe," Wesley challenged. "You're just like the Professor. Loco Leo must be your uncle too."

Travis sneered. "You and the Professor are a real pair."

"Why don't you stop trying to be the big man," I called out. I knew Travis might start on me, but I was angry and didn't care. I wanted to say some of the things I had always thought about Travis. "You're always trying to push somebody around. You're always trying to be the big shot. Well, you're nothing."

Travis stepped toward me. I took two steps backwards and prepared to get hit or pushed. "You better shut your face, Slocombe," he growled. "Or you'll be down with the Professor, wiping your bloody nose, too."

"Yeah, if somebody says something or does something you don't like, you've got to punch them out. But you always make sure they're smaller than you. Somebody like Abe. That's why you don't want Abe to play ball, because he's better than you."

"The Professor ain't nothing. The only thing he can do is brag about Philly and all the great things he can do. Well, he can't do nothing."

"At least he's not afraid like you."

"Yeah? And what am I afraid of?"

"You were afraid to go to the back of the Baker

Mine. You made fun of Abe because he wouldn't go to the back of the mine. Well, he's been to the back of the mine, all the way to the back."

Travis, Wesley, and Skip all laughed. "He's never gone to the back of the mine," Wesley snorted. "He ran out of there before we were halfway back."

I shook my head. "He went to the back. I know because I went with him. We went to the back of both tunnels. Just a couple of weeks ago."

"You're a liar," Travis muttered. "Nobody's been to the back of the right tunnel. Not since Jake and his buddies got buried back there."

"Abe and I have."

"Sure you have."

"I can prove it. If you've got the guts to go in."

"How can you prove it, Slocombe? You're just blowing hot air."

"There's a pile of four rocks at the very back of each tunnel. We put them there."

Travis studied me a moment. "Anybody could put a pile of rocks back there."

I nodded. "But how would I know they were there unless I'd gone back in there? They're there, all right. You could see for yourself if you weren't chicken to go in and look."

"I ain't chicken," Travis bragged. "And someday I'm going to go to the back of that old mine and see if there are any rocks stacked there. And if there aren't . . . "

"Why don't you go up there today and see? But you don't want to go because you're afraid. You can sneak around dumping horse manure all over an old guy's front porch while he's away. Sure, you can do that. But you wouldn't have the guts to do it if he was here. You can push Abe around because he's smaller than you. You can brag about going to the back of the mine someday. But you're afraid to walk up there right now."

He shook his head. "I don't have a flashlight. You can't go in there without a flashlight. Of course, you and the Professor probably walked all the way to the back of the mine without a flashlight. Right?"

I shook my head. "No, we had a flashlight." I stared at him. "I can get you a flashlight. I'll go up with you. I'd like to see *you* go into the mine."

For a long while Travis stared at me without speaking. He was angry. I could tell because his face had turned red and his eyes were dark and glaring and his mouth was closed tight. "I'll go. Today," he announced.

Wesley and Skip looked over at him. They were not smiling any more.

"Go get your flashlight, Slocombe," Travis ordered.

"You won't go," I challenged.

"We'll go." He looked over at the other two. "We ain't afraid, are we?"

"They haven't gone to the back of the mine," Wesley said worriedly. "They're lying."

Travis nodded and swallowed. "Probably. But we're going to take a look. And if those rocks aren't there, Slocombe," he threatened, pointing a finger at me, "what I did to the Professor ain't nothing like what I'm going to do to you."

"And I'll help him," Wesley joined in.

"But I want you there," Travis said. "I want you close by when I find out that there's no pile of rocks."

"Come on," I said to Abe, who was still sitting on the ground. "Let's get a flashlight." I turned back to the others. "Wait for us here. Don't get scared and run off."

"We'll be here, Slocombe."

I started home on a run, and I could hear Abe behind me. I didn't want to go to the mine again. I was scared. But I knew Travis and the others were scared too. They didn't want to go either. But I had been in the mine once. I could go in again.

"Jared," Abe called to me, "wait up."

I slowed down to a walk, and Abe panted up beside me. "Leo said we shouldn't go in there again."

"They're the ones going in."

He shook his head. "But it's dangerous."

"Travis won't dare go in. He's chicken. He's always been a chicken."

I started running again. I didn't stop until I had cut across the corral, climbed the fence, and stood panting behind the hay stack by the barn.

"What's the matter, Jared?" Megan asked suddenly, coming around the corner of the hay stack in her patched pants and faded T-shirt. She stopped at the corner and stared at me.

Abe was just climbing over the corral fence. "Hi, Abe," Megan greeted him. "What are you and Jared doing today?"

"Meg," I said to her, "run to the house and get Mom's red flashlight, the one that's in the kitchen drawer. But don't tell her what you're doing."

"What do you need the flashlight for?"

"Meg, don't ask any questions."

"Can I go with you?" Megan asked. I shook my head. "But I want to go too."

"Not today."

"I'll tell Mom," she threatened.

I hesitated. "Meg, just this once, help me," I pleaded.

Megan frowned and then slowly walked to the house. When she returned, she handed the flashlight to me without saying anything.

I turned to Abe. "Are you coming?"

He thought a moment. "I'll walk up," he answered. "But I'm not going in there again. Nobody should."

I ignored his warning. "Let's go."

Chapter 14

Travis and the others were waiting when we returned. Nobody said much as we cut across the foot of the mountain through the sage and cedar and hiked toward the old mine road and on up the mountain.

At the pond we rested a moment and took a drink. Travis was the first to start up the trail again. "Let's go," he ordered. "We don't have time to hang around here."

Just before we reached the granite wall guarding the upper canyon, Skip looked back down the canyon and protested, "I don't know about this, Travis. These guys are lying to us. Slocombe and the Professor would never dare go in the mine."

Travis turned to me.

"You'd like to believe we didn't," I came back before he could speak. "You don't want to go in there and find out for yourselves because you're afraid."

"We're going," Travis said.

"But, Travis . . . " Skip whined.

"Shut up!" Travis snapped.

We scrambled up the ore slide in front of the mine and stopped, our chests heaving and our mouths sucking in huge gulps of air. I pulled Mom's flashlight from my pocket and held it out to Travis. He stared at it without taking it.

"You've never been to the back of that mine," he said. "No one has."

I didn't answer.

"A guy can't even go down the right tunnel. It's blocked off. You're lying."

"It only looks like it's blocked off. There's a passage over the top. Go in and see for yourself. If there isn't a hole through, then you'll know that I was lying and you won't have to go any further."

Still Travis wouldn't take the flashlight.

"You're real brave," I taunted, "when you're hanging dead cats or spreading horse manure on an old man's porch when he's not around. You're a real tough guy when you're pushing around somebody like Abe. Now let's see . . ."

"Shut your face," he shouted, snatching the flashlight from my hand and giving me a shove. Jabbing a finger in my face, he warned, "You better hope those rocks are there." He turned to the others. "Let's go."

Wesley stepped forward, but Skip hung back. "Come on!" Travis ordered. Skip stared at Travis, his face a sickly white.

"I don't think they went in," Skip whimpered.

"That's what we're going to find out. Come on!"

I guess I hadn't really expected them to enter the mine because when they disappeared into the blackness, I felt an uneasiness creep over me. Anxiously I began pacing back and forth while Abe found a fallen tree and sat down.

"We should have listened to Leo," Abe remarked. "We shouldn't be here."

I didn't answer. I felt sick inside. Walking closer to the mine, I tried to pierce the darkness, but I could see nothing. "How long do you suppose they've been in there?" I asked, rubbing the palms of my hands on my pant legs.

He coughed and clasped his hands together. "I hate this place, Jared."

"They'll make it," I said. "We made it."

There was a faint shudder. I looked around, not knowing if I was imagining things or if the trembling was real. I glanced at Abe. He was looking around too. "What was that?" I asked in a whisper.

He shook his head.

The minutes ticked by as both of us paced in front of the mine. "They've been gone a long time," I mumbled.

"What if something—"

Even while he spoke I felt the earth tremble and heard a faint groan from deep within the mine. My mouth and throat were dry, and my stomach twisted and lurched inside me. "What was that?" I asked.

"There's a light!" Abe cried.

I peered into the mine. In the distant darkness I spotted a tiny pinprick of light bobbing up and down.

Another rumble echoed through the mountain's stomach, and dust and bits of fine rock sprinkled down at the entrance of the mine. I was sure that the whole mountain would split open.

Even before I spotted Travis and Wesley, I could tell by the bobbing light that they were running frantically for the entrance to the mine. I heard them shout as they stumbled along, bumping into each other, scrambling for the safety of daylight.

Suddenly Wesley burst from the dust and darkness. Travis was right behind him. They stumbled out and dropped to their hands and knees.

"It's falling in!" Travis gasped. "We've got to get out of here. The whole mountain's going to fall in. That place *is* haunted. We went past the cave-in. We heard the screams. And then everything started coming down."

"Where's Skip?" I asked, squinting into the mine.

Travis and Wesley gaped about. Skip Manning wasn't with them.

"He was right behind me," Travis said, springing to his feet and screaming into the black hole, "Skip! Skip! Where are you, Skip?" He turned back to us.

"I thought he was just a few feet behind me." He swallowed. "He was right behind me!" he insisted.

"When was he behind you?" I asked, my voice cracking.

"When we were in the right tunnel, when everything started coming down."

"Did he make it out of the right tunnel?" Abe asked, his eyes wide.

Travis shook his head. "I don't know. Everything was coming down. I almost got caught under it. The right tunnel's completely closed off now. I know that. I almost didn't make it out."

"You mean Skip might still be in the right tunnel?" I asked.

"I don't remember him coming out of the right tunnel. But I'm not sure. Maybe he did. Skip! Skip!" he shouted into the mine.

The only answer was a distant rumble from deep inside the mountain.

"We've got to get help!" Travis cried. "We've got to get help." Travis started walking backwards from the mouth of the mine.

"Wait!" Abe shouted. Travis stopped. Abe stared into the mine. "We can't leave him," he said.

"I'm not going in there again!" Wesley burst out. "If he's in there, we'll never get him out. We've got to get somebody else to help."

"Maybe he made it through the hole," I said hopefully. "Maybe he's not trapped in the right tunnel."

"We're going for help," Travis shouted, his voice filled with fear and panic.

"We can't leave him!" Abe screamed. "You can't leave somebody buried in a mine."

But Travis and Wesley weren't listening. Stumbling and falling, they charged down the ore slide.

"There's the other opening," Abe called out. "Leo told us about it."

Rushing after Travis and Wesley, I called to them, "Wait up! Stop!"

Travis and Wesley stopped and turned as Abe and I sprinted after them. "There's another way into the right tunnel," I yelled. "Leo told us about it." I was scared. My stomach was twisting and turning inside me.

"Leo told us that the east mine drops down into the right tunnel," I explained, my voice shaking. "If Skip is trapped in the right tunnel, maybe we can still get him out."

"Leo's a crazy old man," Wesley whimpered. "He doesn't know anything."

"He knows," I insisted. "We have to at least try."

"Who's going in there?" Travis asked.

No one volunteered.

"Will you go in?" Abe asked me.

"I know where the other mine is."

Abe's eyes filled with panic. A tiny muscle twisted above his left eye, and his face was tight. "We can't leave him buried in the mine."

"Let's go," I ordered. "All of us."

"There's nothing we can do," Travis came back. "And it's your fault," he accused me. "You're the one who made us go in there." His hands trembled, and his face was white and drawn. "I'm never going in there again. That place is haunted."

"There aren't any ghosts," I argued. "Abe and I went in." I shrugged. "There wasn't anything."

"I'm not going back to that mine. We're going for help."

"We can't leave Skip," Abe said firmly. "I'll go." Turning to me, he said, "You'll have to show me where the other mine is."

"This is all your fault, Slocombe," Travis accused again.

I knew he was right. How would I ever explain this to Mom and Dad after all the warnings they had given me? How could I explain this to Skip's parents? I felt a terrible weakness in my legs. "You can at least wait for us for a few minutes," I said to Travis and Wesley. "We'll go in. But you have to wait for us."

"There isn't another way in. Leo's crazy. Skip's buried in there, and it's your fault," Travis yelled.

"Just wait!" I screamed. "If he is trapped, a few more minutes won't matter."

Travis stared and gulped. He glanced back toward the mine and nodded. "But just for a few minutes."

Abe and I started back up the mountain, this time detouring around the main mine and going to the east. "I think I can still find it," I said.

"You've got to find it, Jared. It's Skip's only chance," Abe came back.

After we had walked a couple hundred yards, I stopped and pointed. "I think that's the place, straight ahead where you see the clump of brush to the right of the pine trees. The mine entrance is behind those bushes."

"Let's go," Abe whispered.

"What if the old mine has caved in?" I asked.

"We've got to find Skip," was Abe's only answer.

I looked back. Travis and Wesley had started to follow us.

Abe started forward. I took his arm. "If the old mine looks bad, we can't go in."

Abe pulled his arm free without answering and started toward the brush. I hesitated a moment and then followed. The brush was thick. Abe and I fought our way through it, the branches tugging at our arms and legs. Finally we pushed through. At the base of the orange rock was a small opening about four feet wide that dropped steeply into the ground.

Abe turned to me. "Give me the light." He

snatched the flashlight as I held it out and started into the opening.

Grabbing his arm, I pleaded, "Abe, wait! Let's—"

"What if you were in there?" he asked, ripping his arm away from me.

"Wait!" I grabbed him again. He tore his arm free, hitting me in the face with a flying elbow that knocked me backward. Holding the side of my face, I watched Abe climb down through the opening. I hesitated only a moment and then followed him.

The tunnel was low and narrow and we had to hunch over, groping our way along the cold, jagged walls of the old mine, clinging to the dim yellow light the flashlight cast in front of us.

The tunnel dropped steeply and to the left. Before we had gone more than a hundred feet the entrance disappeared and we were locked in the blackness.

"Abe!" I rasped. "Abe, I don't know if we should . . ."

"The walls are strong," Abe whispered back. He directed the light onto the rough walls. "Look. It's not like the mine below. It won't give way."

I don't know how far we walked. It seemed forever and the direction of the tunnel was always down. The air was stale and musty. The tromp of our feet made a dull, muffled sound as we stumbled along.

"Maybe we shouldn't go any further," I whispered.

Abe stopped and held up his hand. "Listen!" he whispered.

I stopped and held my breath, straining to hear. "It's the water!" I gasped. "It's the underground creek."

We started forward again. Fifty yards farther on there was a jagged seam in the rock along the left wall of the tunnel. It had pulled apart and left an opening little more than two feet wide. We could hear the rush of water inside.

"This must be the place," Abe ventured, shining the light inside. He peered intently. "I can see the water."

He pressed through the opening. More than anything I wanted to turn around and go back.

"It opens up," Abe called back to me. "The water's washed a regular tunnel through here, just like Leo said. Come on, Jared. We can make it. We're right above the other mine."

I followed Abe. The floor of the passage was wet, and the rock walls were cold and damp. The water splashed along on our right and then disappeared through the opening that dropped into the main mine. We crept forward. Abe shone the light down through the opening. The drop wasn't nearly as steep as I had thought it would be, and we managed to climb down with little trouble.

When we finally stood in the tunnel of the main mine, I shivered. "Where do you think he is?" I asked.

He glanced once toward the back of the mine and then nodded to the front. "Travis said he was right behind him. He must be this way."

We started walking, my heart pounding in my chest until I ached. My breath came in short, tight gasps. As we walked along I noticed fresh piles of dirt and rock that had broken free from above. We walked almost to the old cave-in, and then Abe stopped abruptly and cried, "Skip! Is that you, Skip?"

Skip Manning was lying face down on the floor of the mine, his legs partially covered with dirt and rock. He groaned and whimpered, "Don't leave me. Please don't leave me, Travis."

Both of us rushed forward and dropped to our knees beside him. "Are his legs caught?" Abe directed the light toward Skip's legs, which were buried beneath a pile of rock and dirt. A beam had fallen and caught Skip's left leg just below the knee.

Abe thrust the flashlight toward me and began to dig with his hands. I watched him for a moment and then, setting the light on the ground, I joined him. All the while Skip held a bleeding bump on his head and whimpered crazily.

Finally we removed enough of the rock and dirt so that Abe and I could lift the beam just enough to pull Skip free. While Abe grunted and strained against the wooden beam, I grabbed Skip under the arms and pulled. "Lift harder, Abe!" I cried, blinking back tears of frustration and fear.

"Keep pulling," Abe ordered between clenched teeth.

I pulled again, and slowly I managed to work Skip free.

"Get me out of here," Skip sobbed. "Oh, please, Travis, get me out."

"Come on, Abe, let's go. Let's get out of here before the whole mountain falls in on us!"

Abe and I held Skip between us, each of us with one of Skip's arms draped around our necks. We held him up, half dragging half pulling him along. I was glad Skip was small. Had he been any bigger, we could never have gotten him out.

Skip's head and leg were hurting him, and he groaned, calling out to Travis, begging him not to leave him behind. The hard part was getting Skip through the hole where the creek washed through the side of the mine. I climbed up first, and then Abe helped push Skip up while I pulled with all my might.

All the time we were stumbling along, I expected the mine to fall in on us. I kept praying that we would make it. And then suddenly we were scrambling through the tangle of brush that covered the entrance to the mine.

In the daylight I looked at Skip. He had a huge

bloody bump on his forehead. His eyes were closed, and his pale face was streaked with dirt and tears.

Travis and Wesley were still waiting. When they saw us, they charged toward us.

"We'll take him down the mountain from here," Wesley volunteered, stepping forward and grabbing Skip. Travis followed. Picking him up, the two of them started down the mountain.

"Are you all right?" I asked Abe, who stood wide-eyed and panting.

He glanced back toward the mine, and I thought I heard another rumble deep inside the mountain. "Let's get out of here," he said, turning back to me.

Abe and I let Travis and Wesley take Skip down the mountain. We hung back, taking our time to climb down the mountain in silence.

When I reached home, I went straight to the barn to begin the afternoon milking, hoping to erase the terrible memories of the afternoon. I was just finishing milking the first cow when Megan burst into the barn and announced breathlessly, "Mom's looking for you. She's been calling like mad for you."

I stared at her.

"I didn't say a thing, Jared. Honest."

"Why's she looking for me?"

Megan didn't have time to respond, but I had my answer when Mom rushed into the barn. Stopping in the doorway, she looked around, first at me, then at the cows, and finally at the bucket of milk at my feet. For a moment she struggled to catch her breath, and then she sighed with relief, "You gave me a fright, Son."

"Me?" I asked, trying to conceal my guilt.

"I'm glad to see you're milking. I was afraid that . . . " She closed her eyes and took a deep breath. "They brought Skip Manning down the mountain a while back. He was almost buried in the old mine. They took him to the hospital in Fairview. I thought maybe you had been with those boys. I wondered if maybe you were still up there."

"I'm just milking, Mom," I mumbled, trying not to lie.

Pressing her lips together, Mom turned and left the barn. I glanced over at Megan. She shook her head. "I didn't say anything."

"Thanks, Meg," I whispered.

"What happened?" she inquired, creeping close to me. "Did you see the ghosts?"

"I don't want to talk about it, Meg. Not today. Maybe never. I've got chores to do."

Chapter 15

The next day as I sat next to Mom and the girls waiting for sacrament meeting to begin, I still felt numb. I hadn't said anything to Mom, and although Megan suspected something and pestered me with questions, I refused to talk to her about what had happened.

I had had a terrible night, sleeping restlessly, not quite able to shake the awful feeling that I was trapped deep inside the mountain's belly while hundreds of tons of rock and dirt crashed down upon me. For the first time in years I kept the night-light on next to my bed. I didn't want to be in the dark any more.

I thought a lot about Abe. I wanted to speak to him. He was the only one who would understand what I was feeling.

"Brothers and sisters," Uncle Josh began speaking from the pulpit, "I want to welcome you to our sacrament meeting." He paused a moment and gazed out over the congregation. "We have reason to be especially thankful today. Most of you are probably aware that our little community had a brush with disaster yesterday. Some of our young men went up the mountain and began exploring in the old Baker Mine."

I gazed intently at Uncle Josh. Megan reached over slyly and put her hand in mine.

"Part of the old mine collapsed, and Skip Manning almost lost his life. His folks tell me that he'll be all right, though. He should be coming home from the hospital this afternoon. He has some bumps and bruises and a terrible knot on his head. For a while it looked as if his leg had been broken, but it will be okay as soon as the swelling and the soreness leave. The doctors think he'll be all right."

Uncle Josh cleared his throat. "If it hadn't been for the quick thinking and action of Travis Williams and Wesley Payton, Skip might not have made it down the mountain. They're the ones who brought him down, probably risking their lives to help their friend. Hopefully this will help us realize how dangerous those old mines . . . "

I didn't listen any more. Travis and Wesley risked their lives? I couldn't believe what I was hearing. But they had been the ones who had carried Skip down the mountain. Skip probably didn't remember anything. Travis and Wesley would have explained what had happened. Although I didn't want Mom to know that I had been inside the old mine, I did want to do something about not giving Travis and Wesley credit for what someone else had done.

Suddenly I couldn't concentrate. I was the only one in the chapel who actually knew what had happened at the Baker Mine. Halfway through sacrament meeting I whispered to Mom that I needed a drink. Once out of the chapel, I left the building and began walking home.

Passing Leo's place on my way, I spotted him in back, loading his black truck with scrap metal. Abe was there helping. For a moment I watched, and then I turned up the cracked front walk and went to where they were working.

Abe glanced in my direction as I approached. "Aren't you supposed to be in church?" he asked as he threw a rusty metal bar into the back of the truck. "I thought you always went."

"I didn't feel like staying today. I wish yesterday had never happened." I wet my lips. "Did you sleep last night?" I asked.

He looked at me and then shrugged. "I kept thinking. About my dad." He turned away. "I know they didn't leave him in that mine back in Pennsylvania. They would have helped him, just like I knew I had to help Skip."

"I didn't sleep much at all," I remarked.

"Were you scared?"

I thought a moment. "Sure." I shrugged. "Not of

ghosts, if that's what you mean. There aren't ghosts up there. At least not like we used to believe. I don't believe in ghosts."

"Maybe you've got ghosts all around you down here and don't even know it," Leo muttered.

"Ghosts around me here?" I questioned

"A ghost is anything you're afraid of."

"I didn't say I was afraid last night. I just said I couldn't sleep much. I kept thinking about getting stuck in that mine and not ever getting out again. I was just worried."

"You get tired of church today?" Leo asked me, slapping his hands against his pant legs to clean off the dusty rust clinging there.

I shook my head. "I just didn't want to stay today."

Abe threw a twisted metal post into the back of the truck. "I thought maybe after yesterday you were coming for me," he commented, turning toward me. "To see if I'd go to church with you." He smiled faintly and then shrugged. "I used to think it wouldn't be so bad to go if someone came for me." He stared down at the ground. He smiled, a sad smile. "In Philly, people—" He stopped and shook his head. "In Philly, people used to come for me. I kinda liked that. But I'm not in Philly, and I don't wait for anyone to come any more."

"They think Travis and Wesley saved Skip," I

burst out. I swallowed and looked at Abe. "Everybody thinks Travis and Wesley saved Skip's life."

Abe shrugged, indifferent.

"But *they* left him. They didn't go back for him. They would have charged down the mountain if I hadn't stopped them."

"What difference does it make? He got out."

"But it's not fair. You were the one that made us go into the mine. You saved Skip, not them. I couldn't ever have done it, not without you. The first time we went into the mine . . . " I paused. "I would never have gone if you hadn't been with me."

"That's what friends are for, to help each other when one's in a fix. A friend always comes for you when you need him."

"Maybe," I muttered. "But," I added angrily, "Travis and Wesley shouldn't be the heroes. They ran."

Abe and Leo continued to work.

"I'm going home," I said, shaking my head. "I can't go back to church today. I don't know if I ever want to go back there with them."

"I thought you were going to be made a deacon in a couple of weeks."

"Maybe I won't."

Abe shrugged and stared intently at the ground for a long time without speaking. I turned and headed home, feeling terribly cheated and alone.

I walked out by the corral and sat on the fence, watching the cows chew their cuds and flick flies with their tails. I wanted to block everything from my mind because it frustrated me too much to think. But my mind was crammed full of thoughts, all of them demanding my attention. And then one thought clambered above the rest. It was something Leo had said a few minutes earlier, something about not all my ghosts being in the Baker Mine. And then I realized what should have been so obvious: my real ghosts had never been in the mine; they were still around me. Travis and Wesley were two of them. And they were real. I wasn't just afraid of what they could do to me. I was afraid of what they thought and what they would make others think. That was the reason I had punched the old burlap bag in the basement of the school. It was only there, alone and away from all the staring eyes, that I could be brave, that I could tell myself that nothing frightened me.

But I hadn't been alone! Even down in the basement, when I felt my greatest courage, Abe had been there. He had made me believe that maybe, just maybe, I didn't have to back down from Travis and Wesley. Maybe I could stand up to them. When I went to Leo's place to get the milk bucket, Abe had gone with me. Both times I had gone into the mine, I had had the courage to go inside because Abe was there.

I ducked my head in shame as I sat contemplating the corral fence. I had never claimed Abe as a friend. Even to Megan I had refused to actually say he was my friend because I had been afraid of what people would think. And yet, suddenly, I realized that he was the best friend I had.

I jumped down from the fence, remembering what Abe had said: "A friend is always there when you're in a fix. A friend always comes for you."

"I came for you," I said quietly to Abe as I walked up behind him and Leo. They were loading the last few pieces of rusty metal and hadn't heard or seen me coming this time. Abe turned around and stared.

"You said you'd go if someone came for you."

"To church?" Abe asked, surprised.

I shrugged. "To anyplace. But to church right now."

"I thought you weren't going again."

"I didn't want to be there alone."

"Maybe it's easier for me to stay here," he said. "Easier for both of us."

"Maybe friends shouldn't always choose the easiest way. The easiest way isn't always the best way."

"What do you mean?"

I thought a moment. "It would have been easiest not to go back for Skip. But that wasn't the best way." I took a long, deep breath and let the air out slowly.

"I'm sorry I didn't come sooner. You will come, won't you?"

Abe turned to Leo, who gazed on in silence. "Go on. I can take care of things here," he finally said.

"I'd have to change my clothes."

"I'll wait for you."

Abe hesitated only a moment, and then he followed me. I took several steps and then turned back to Leo. "Do you want to come?" I asked.

A strange, disbelieving smile curled across Leo's crooked mouth. "Maybe if someone had come for me years ago, I would have gone. But it's too late. No one would want me there now."

"How about if we come for you next week?" I asked, smiling slightly. "Friends always come for you."

Sacrament meeting was over when Abe and I walked into the church. I knew it would be. I stared down the long hall to my classroom, the last room on the right.

Slowly I walked down the hall, feeling my heart pound in my chest. At the end of the hall I pushed open the door and stepped inside. Abe followed.

Brother Marshall was giving a lesson on the Good Samaritan, but he stopped when I entered. Every eye turned toward us. Travis was there. So was Wesley. So were others.

"I was wondering where you were, Jared," Brother

Marshall greeted me with a smile. "Who's the young man with you?"

I cleared my throat. "This is—" My voice cracked. I swallowed and tried again. "This is—Abraham."

Travis and Wesley snickered.

I felt my cheeks redden just a little. I turned to Abe and spoke again, more loudly this time. "This is Abraham O'Hara, a friend of mine."

"He's really the Professor," Travis grinned, leaning back in his chair.

"He's Abraham O'Hara," I corrected, my face burning and my mouth dry. "He'll be coming with me from now on."

The next day at school I waited for the last bell to ring. When it did, everyone jumped for the door, the boys all heading for the ball diamond. We had planned to play a big game that day, sort of a championship game. We'd talked about it for several days, each side bragging about winning.

I stayed in my seat as the others rushed out. I glanced across the aisle. Abe was still hunched over his desk, finishing an English paper that wasn't due for two more days. "You going to play with us today?" I asked.

He stared across the aisle at me. "I was figuring on finishing this paper." He turned back to his desk. "And I've got some reading to do."

"I'd like you to play with us. We could really use

you today." I pushed myself to my feet, started for the door and then stopped. "We'll go out together," I said, turning.

"They won't let me play."

"Today you play. From now on you don't sit on the back steps alone."

Abe studied me a moment. Slowly he set his pencil down, gathered his books, and joined me.

When Abe and I arrived, my team was getting ready to take the field. "Abe's playing on my team," I spoke up so everyone could hear.

"Our team's already one short," Travis came back matter-of-factly, almost ignoring me. "Skip's gone."

"I guess we'll have uneven teams." I sensed all eyes on me. Abe was standing a few steps away. "He plays," I insisted.

Travis laughed and turned to the others on my team. "Which one of you guys is sitting out so the Professor can play?"

They didn't answer. But they didn't laugh either, and I think Travis had expected them to laugh or to protest. They waited for me—just like they always waited for me.

"He doesn't have a glove," Travis objected.

"He can use mine," I said, tossing Abe my glove. "I'll borrow someone else's."

"I said he'll make the teams uneven," Travis argued.

"You can choose someone else from our team to play with you."

"All right, we'll take Reg."

"I'm playing with Jared," Reg said.

"Fine," Travis shrugged. "Then the Professor doesn't play."

"Abe will pitch," I answered. "Reg can play where he wants."

"I'll play with you, Jared," Reg repeated.

"And I'm playing with Jared and Abe," Chris Winder called out.

Travis strutted toward me, glaring. Wesley followed him. "Who said you could call the shots?" Wesley growled at me, stepping in front of Travis. "You two almost got us killed Saturday. Do you think you're going to call the shots after that?" Suddenly he pushed me, knocking me a couple of steps backward.

I staggered and then quickly steadied myself. "Abe plays," I said, my voice shaking just a little. "We should have let him play a long time ago."

"We didn't want him playing before, and we sure don't want him playing now, not after what you two did Saturday." Wesley started toward me, his fists clenched at his sides. I took one step backward and then held my ground, bringing my fists up in front of me.

Wesley stopped. Travis laughed. "All right, Wesley, if he wants it that way, give it to him. He's a wimp."

Wesley glanced from Travis to me and then started to laugh. "Old Slocombe thinks he's a tough guy," he said to Travis. "The Professor probably taught him."

I felt my mouth dry out, and my heart thumped in my chest until I thought it was going to hammer right through my ribs. Travis had always beaten me, and I was sure that Wesley, being bigger and stronger, could beat Travis. I felt a sick weakening in the pit of my stomach. I didn't want to fight. I wanted to turn and run. But I knew deep inside me that this was one time I couldn't walk away. Even if I got punched and beaten, I couldn't run. This was a ghost I had to face. I was all alone against Wesley and Travis.

"Come on, Jared, you can do it," Abe shouted behind me. "Do it just like we practiced." I glanced over at him, surprised. "Nobody can beat you. Keep your guard up and work your left jab. Wait for him to open up and then come through with your right. You can do it, Jared. I know you can!"

I felt a lightness in my head as I suddenly realized that I wasn't alone. Abe was there. My jaw clamped tight, and I began to circle away from Wesley, who was moving in toward me.

"Get up on your toes," Abe coached me. "Keep moving. Wait for him to make his move. You can do it, Jared. I know you can."

"Shut up, Professor!" Travis growled. "Unless you want to jump in there with them."

In that moment I made my move. I circled to my right and stepped back. Wesley charged toward me. I faked a backward step and then shot forward, lashing out with a left jab. Wesley had expected me to stay away from him, even run. I caught him completely off guard. Putting his fists up, he tried to protect his face, but two of my quick jabs grazed his cheek and chin, stunning him. He dropped his guard just a little, and I came across with my right, smashing him on the side of his face. Groaning, he stumbled back, shaking his head.

I wet my lips and swallowed. The knuckles on my right fist throbbed where they had banged against Wesley's head. My head felt light as I studied Wesley. He shook his head and glowered at me while he rubbed the side of his head. "Okay, Slocombe, you're mine now."

My knees felt weak. I wasn't sure if I could hold Wesley off again, not now that he was mad.

"You've got him, Jared," Abe coached. "Just wait for the right time. Do what we practiced. Nobody can get you."

Wesley threw up his fists and charged toward me, flailing his arms wildly. I danced out of his way and threw two quick jabs that jarred him upright. He charged again. I faked a left. He ducked slightly and opened up his whole left side. I hit him with a hard, quick punch that smashed into his nose, sending him sprawling backwards.

As soon as he hit the ground, he sat up, grabbing his nose, which had sprung a red trickle down over his lips and onto his chin. He pulled his bloody hand away and studied it, as though unable to understand what had happened to him. He looked up at me, then at Travis, and finally back at his hand.

I remained a few feet away from him with my fists still up. Slowly a warm confidence flooded over me. I knew that it didn't matter how many times Wesley got up, I could beat him. *We* could beat him, Abe and I! I guess Wesley figured the same thing because he wiped his bloody hand on his pants and stood up, this time without charging at me. His shoulders were hunched a bit, and he studied me warily.

"I didn't want to fight you," I said. I glanced over at Abe. "But Abe's playing."

"Good job, Jared," I heard Reg whisper behind me.

Travis was staring at Wesley as though unable to understand what had just happened. He glanced at me, knowing that he had easily beaten me before. I think he knew I was different now.

"Okay," Travis muttered, "the Professor can play. But it won't help you any. We're still going to beat you, with or without the Professor." He turned and started toward home plate, Wesley following a step or two behind him.

"Wait," I called out. Travis stopped and turned around. "His name is Abraham," I announced, louder than I had intended to. I looked around the circle of faces because I was speaking to everyone now. "Abraham O'Hara. His friends can call him Abe." I swallowed. "But from now on nobody calls him Professor."

"Says who?" Travis challenged.

I walked over to him. "I say so," I answered quietly.

Travis glared at me and then glanced quickly at Wesley who was staring at the ground, still holding his nose. Travis started to turn away and I grabbed his arm. "His name is Abraham," I repeated.

"I heard you."

"And he's one of us. He's better than any of us."

"What makes you think so?" Travis sneered.

I swallowed and took a quick breath. "You didn't save Skip," I accused. "I don't care what everybody else thinks."

"Wesley and I brought him down the mountain. He'd still be up there if we hadn't packed him down with us."

"You left him in the mine. You got scared and left him trapped in the mine. He'd still be there. Dead. Nobody except Abe dared go in after him."

I looked around the circle of faces. "I knew Skip

was trapped in the mine. But I didn't want to go in after him. The whole place was caving in. Wesley and Travis ran. I wanted to run too because I was scared."

I took a deep breath and looked at Abe. "Abe was scared too." I shook my head. "But he didn't run. He went back in the mine. I followed him."

All eyes turned toward Abe, whose cheeks were burning red while he stared at the ground. "Abe was the one who went in the mine and found Skip and dug him out." Turning back to Travis, I said, "You were able to take Skip down the mountain because Abe first went in and dragged him out of the mine. Isn't that true?"

"How should I know? Everything was happening so fast."

I shrugged. "You wouldn't know because you ran away." I shook my head. "But not Abe. Isn't that right?" I asked Travis.

He didn't answer.

"Isn't that right, Wesley?"

Wesley looked up at me and then glanced over at Abe. "We didn't go back in the mine looking for Skip," he mumbled, still rubbing his nose. "Somebody else brought Skip out of the mine. Travis and I just carried him down the mountain."

"Abe brought him out of the mine. Abe saved Skip's life. And from now on he doesn't sit on the back steps and watch the rest of us play. He plays with us, whenever he wants."

I turned back to my team. Every one of them was smiling at Abe. Reg reached out and touched Abe's shoulder. "Way to go, Abe," he whispered.

"Come on, Abe," Chris called out. "Pitch another game like you did last time. We'll skunk 'em."

"Come on, Abe," Reg shouted. "You can do it."

As I walked to my position at first base, I glanced toward the pitcher's mound. Abe and I exchanged nods. And then we both smiled. I didn't know what the score would be at the end of the game, but I did know that we had already won.